JIMMY THREEPWOOD AND THE ECHOES OF THE PAST

By

RICH PITMAN

JIMMY THREEPWOOD AND THE ECHOES OF THE PAST

By

RICH PITMAN

Cover design by Vixydesign

Published by

Crimson Cloak Publishing

ISBN 13: 978-1-68160-733-7

ISBN 10: 1-68160-733-6

Edited by Denna Holm

Publisher's Publication in Data

Pitman, Rich

Jimmy Threepwood and the Echoes of the Past

1. Fiction 2. Fantasy 3. Young Adult

For Marnie Diana Pitman, my whirlwind inside the chaos.

CHAPTER 1

The Rise of Imjimn-Ra....

Mara Jenkins wiped the sweat from her forehead with a handkerchief as she stared out at the endless sheet of sand sparkling like a carpet of gold under the bright sunlight. Heat radiated through her long blonde hair tied up at the back of her head. Grains of sand seeped through her worn leather ankle boots, past her socks, to scour her bare skin.

After nearly six months on this expedition, they had finally stumbled upon a towering, awe-inspiring Egyptian pyramid. With mounting pressure from the Graveman Brothers—their financiers—threatening to pull the plug on their project, the find had not come a moment too soon.

With her stomach abuzz with excitement, Mara removed a crumpled map from the rear pocket of her shorts, frowning as she studied it. *I just don't understand it. This area has been checked and rechecked since records began ... and nothing. This pyramid shouldn't exist. It just doesn't make any sense.* She folded the map and put it back into her pocket.

"Mara," a voice shouted from behind, snapping her from her thoughts.

She spun around, shielding her eyes from the sun, to find Rex, her long-time expedition companion, dressed in his cargo shorts, dirty white shirt and a tan cowboy hat, in a heated argument with a local Egyptian guide.

"What do you mean it's the tomb of Imjimn-Ra?" Rex shouted, clearly losing his temper as he swatted sand from his bare legs. "How can a pyramid this size be lost for centuries?"

The guide stumbled in the sand and instinctively reached for the red fez balanced on his head. He slapped the black tassel from his eyes and said in broken English, a slight quaver in his tone, "He rises! He rises. It is foretold he will rise. Please, please, we must go. Go now!" He pointed at the foreboding pyramid, his whole body visibly shaking. A small grey monkey perched on his shoulder, wearing a smaller version of his master's hat, also pointed at the pyramid.

The guide grabbed Rex's arm as he reached for the reins of a camel loaded with bags and equipment and tried to lead him back the way they had come.

Rex jerked free of the guide. "Mara, he keeps talking about Imjimn-Ra. What is that? Do you know what he's talking about?"

Mara paused thoughtfully, then grinned, growing even more excited. "It is said that Imjimn-Ra was one of the last of the Egyptian dynasty. Supposedly, he asked to be buried alive inside a tomb to wait for the right time to return. There are cave drawings to depict the story, but little is known except the tomb apparently sank into the sand, never to be found again."

Rubbing her hands together, Mara started to jump up and down, wobbling as she sank into the sand. She grabbed Rex's arm. "Do you think this is it? This could be the greatest archaeological find of our time."

Rex grinned, caught up in her excitement. "We'll be talked about for years!"

"No, no, no!" mumbled the guide, turning to walk away. "I must go. This no good. I must go."

"Taleev wait!" Mara shouted. "Please, please help us. Just help us to open the tomb. We won't go in, and we'll call teams to help us with the dig. Please … it may not even be Imjimn-Ra. It could be anything."

After an awkward silence that seemed to last an eternity, Mara shouted, "We'll pay you double what we agreed. Triple!"

Reluctantly, Taleev stopped and turned to face Mara, keeping his head down. Without looking into her eyes, he nodded. From his shoulder, Lucka, his pet monkey, squawked and clapped his hands together.

The group approached the stepped structure. Mara ran her fingers over the lowest stone step, which stood the same height as her knees. She wiped a thick layer of sand away, finding the jagged stone rough against her skin. But what surprised her most was the temperature, icy-cold even under the roaring desert sun. She pulled her hand back, rubbing her fingertips together before she reached out to touch it again. *Almost like a glacier,* she thought.

The two archaeologists circled the structure in wonder, processing every chip and scratch. Adrenaline coursed through Mara's blood, her excitement building.

Rex stopped periodically to crouch down to use a thin metal knife to scrape the stone into small, transparent plastic bags. "This is amazing," he shouted, rubbing his dirt-covered, stubbly chin. "I've never seen anything like this. As far as I know, this type of stone doesn't exist. It's like a huge slab of ice but with the solid texture of white limestone." He leapt up on the first step and pressed down with his foot. "Wait until the others see this!"

"Rex!" Mara shouted with a sense of urgency. "Rex!"

Jumping down from the step, Rex charged back to where Mara knelt in the sand, running her hands along the stone in front of her.

"Look," she said. "I've found a gap in the stone. Maybe a door. There's a symbol here next to it." She smoothed the sand away from the indented, circular plate to show the image of a large black, fire-breathing serpent.

As they stared intently, mouths hanging open, a freak gust of wind blew past, revealing two more circular serpents, one about a metre away from the gap Mara had found. The third sat high above the other two, forming a triangle. Mara gasped when it started to glow, and a faint static hum filled the air.

The three stepped back and watched in wonder as a thin eclectic-blue line sizzled and connected the sections of the triangle.

"Nooo!" screamed a horrified Taleev, staggering backwards, his hands held out in front of him. It's the symbol of Imjimn-Ra!"

"What is it?" Mara shouted. "Why are you so scared, Taleev?"

Visibly shaking, Taleev said, "Imjimn-Ra will rise from the earth and destroy us all. He shall show no mercy, and the world will be reborn in his image. That is what has been written!"

Before he had time to react, Lucka sprang from Taleev's shoulder and scurried up the face of the pyramid, his body breaking the electrical circuit. The little grey monkey squawked as he reached the top symbol and pressed it. The surge of electrical current launched Lucka through the air and he crashed into the sand.

As Taleev raced to the monkey, the ground below them began to rumble and shake.

Mara jumped back as four giant stone statues burst through the sand, each statue almost as tall as the pyramid. The eyes of the stone sculptures blazed a fiery red, followed by the sound of stone grinding on stone.

With a thunderous crack, the whole structure spread open, revealing a hidden staircase leading down into the darkness.

Without a second thought, Rex and Mara charged down the steps. At the top, dust filled their lungs, and they could smell the dank, stale air leaking from within. Two cloth torches were set on the wall next to the entrance. Rex and Mara wasted no time lighting them. As the flames illuminated the downward staircase, they each took a step and were gone.

Taleev, still clutching Lucka, watched in horror as Rex and Mara entered the sacred tomb. His chest throbbed, his breathing ragged, and he felt like his heart might jump right out of his chest. Holding his fez in place, he pulled Lucka in tight and started to walk away.

Keeping his head down, Taleev grabbed the leather reins of his camel and gave a gentle tug. As he plodded forward, he heard Mara's ecstatic voice ricochet along the passage out into the vast desert.

"It's him! We've found him. We've found Imjimn-Ra!"

Taleev stopped, rubbing his hand over his face. With a deep sigh, he released the reins and carefully crept back to the entrance, more out of curiosity than with thoughts of collecting the king's ransom he'd been promised for helping them.

As he climbed the steps, he could hear the excitement in Rex and Mara's voice. The instant his foot touched the top step, another freak gust of wind swirled past, swiping a layer of sand away from the stone above the doorway.

Gulping nervously, Taleev concentrated on the words, which altered from an unknown language to one he understood.

All should fear the return of the ruler
For the world will meet its demise when
Imjimn-Ra rises from the ashes.

Grabbing the wall for support, Taleev peered into the darkness, barely able to see two silhouettes moving down below. His right hand trembled as grains of stone crumbled beneath his grip.

"Look at these treasures," the distant voice of Mara said. "We'll need to get teams here straight away."

"Look at this workmanship," Rex replied. "Exquisite. The tomb of Imjimn-Ra. What do we do? Shall we open it?"

"No," Mara said. "Remember what Taleev said. I think we need to get more people here, just in case."

"I can't wait!" Rex's voice boomed.

Taleev cringed when he heard the clank of metal being rammed into a stone sarcophagus, followed by the loud scraping of stone on stone. An almighty crash made him jump, and he ducked as a mist of dust and ash swept up the passage from below.

They've broken the seal. Fools! he thought, tasting the decay on the tip of his tongue. *They've pulled off the lid to his resting place. Why do people not listen?*

"He's perfect," Mara said, awe in her tone. "His skin has been preserved better than anything I've ever seen. It's turned brown and is slightly shrivelled, but what a specimen! We're going to be rich."

"I've never seen anything like it, Mara. It looks as though he was mummified, but the wrappings are torn and shredded all over his body. They're just hanging loose."

The air became suddenly oppressive, and an undertone of fear could be heard in Mara's voice when she said, "Rex, it just moved!"

"Don't be silly, Mara."

"It did. I'm sure … look! Its arm just moved."

"BACK! MARA, GET BACK!"

Two shots were fired, then a moment of silence. Taleev held his breath, frozen, his heart in his throat. He jumped again when a scream filled the air. In the flickering light below, he could see the silhouette of a dragon take shape.

Immense, white-hot fire blasted along the passage, exploding out of the entrance, burning Taleev's face before he could dive for cover. The dragon roared as the stench of burned flesh filled the air.

Ignoring his burns, Taleev wasted no time running over to grab the reins of the camel. He scurried off as fast as his legs would carry him, not sticking around to see the dragon morph back into its human form.

CHAPTER 2

The mysterious delivery….

Alone cloaked woman glanced in distress over her shoulder as she splashed through the puddles of water. She scurried along the soaked footpath, the howling wind and rain pounding her face.

The bright headlights of an approaching car forced her to release her two-handed grip on the concealed item tucked under her arm beneath her cloak. Shielding her eyes, she could feel the heavy item digging into her side as the vehicle passed, sending a tidal wave of dirty water onto her feet. In the background, the bay of hounds carried on the wind. Terrified, she glanced behind her, took hold of the package with both hands and picked up the pace. Her eyes darted wildly in every direction as she scurried around the bend, searching for an escape.

Another car raced past, its headlights illuminating the white street sign.

Mountbatten Close

The dogs were getting closer. She turned to look over her shoulder and stubbed her toe on the uneven floor, losing her balance. Her only thought as she fell was to protect the package gripped tightly in her hands. She slammed down hard, scraping her right shoulder and the side of her face, her knuckles shredded. Shaking hard, she pulled herself up and limped on. She was forced to stop to rest on a knee-high wall in the middle of the Close.

To her left was a giant wall with a small patch of green in front of it. It had once been a doorway used by the Gatekeeper. She could feel his evil presence leaking from within. The woman crouched when two males, one wearing a bright yellow coat, walked out of the estate. A car drove into the area behind her, turning off past a row of houses. She made note of all the cars parked in the Close.

Looking ahead, she could see all manner of cars parked in the Close. The house she wanted was tucked away in the corner.

As she hobbled forward in the eerie silence, a cat darted out from under a car and bounded up a grass verge before vaulting a garden fence. Wincing at every breath, the woman checked behind her again. But the Close was empty, filled only with the light from tall silver streetlamps.

*

The stench of burnt magma wafted into Jimmy's nose, stabbing at the back of his throat. The pungent scent crawled down his oesophagus, leaving the distinct taste of copper on his tongue. A jet of purple lightning tore through the blood-red sky above his head, leaving a scar in the atmosphere. The world groaned and grumbled in distress.

When he heard a crunch beneath his boots, Jimmy stopped and glanced down at the dry, lifeless ground. Crouching down, he ran his fingers over the brown, withered stem of a flower. The instant the moisture from his fingers touched it, it snapped and disintegrated into dust which floated away on the breeze.

He sighed at the devastation surrounding him, devastation he had caused. The world remained silent apart from a gushing river of smouldering lava next to where Jimmy walked. His childhood home had once stood here. The river of yellow and black fire had chewed up everything in its wake. All that remained of the area was the giant wall where he had once been taken by the Gatekeeper all those years ago. The bottom right quarter of the wall had disintegrated. All that remained was a singed, fragmented shell.

Sorrow nipped at his mind as he stared at a tree he used to climb in his youth. The once grand tree, filled with magnificence and power, had been reduced to a fragile, lifeless, burnt stump.

High above his head, the disfigured sky screamed in agony again, and droplets of rain began to fall. Jimmy grimaced in pain as the water splashed on his collar-length ginger hair. The material of his black robes sizzled under the acid-like fall. He rubbed the emblem of the golden phoenix on his right breast pocket and started to jog as the droplets turned into a shower, burning his skin.

Taking shelter under the skeleton of an old, abandoned house, he watched as the loathsome rainfall ate into the earth. This wasn't the first time it had rained like this since the purge. He felt empty inside ... and alone.

A flicker of movement caught his attention out of the corner of his eye. The bubbling lava parted as a figure rose from it and staggered forward. With each step, a chunk of the steaming magma fell from its body, leaving behind a sculptured human form and familiar face.

"Dad...!" Jimmy shouted, perplexed. "Dad!"

"Jimmy ... I've learnt to hold my form for longer, but this is the end for me. I've tried everything to escape, but I'm lost. There is no way out for me. But there is still time for you, my

son. What you see here is the destruction that will occur if Tyranacus is released! Nothing will survive. You must find another way. Pleaaseee, Jimmy."

Jimmy held his hand out to him. Seeing his father this way, his friend, felt like a hole had been punched in his heart. Then he heard the familiar creak of a coiled spring as the metal gate to his garden slammed shut.

Snapped out of his dream, Jimmy struggled to take a breath. The ashen stench lingered in the back of his throat as he finally sucked in a giant gasp.

Still shaken by what he had seen, he threw the covers of his bed back and leaned over to part the curtains. *The wall,* he thought, wiping his eyes. Peering to the right, he found the council estate still there, and the wall was intact. Even the tree looked strong and nourished.

He pressed his face against the window, trying to see into the garden. A visitor stood below, impatiently banging the lion-head knocker. He tapped the glass. "Shhhhh," he mumbled, knowing they couldn't hear him. "You'll wake my mother up." He scrambled off the bed and clambered down the stairs, his hand squeaking from friction on the wooden banister.

Jimmy cracked the door open, but the wind caught it and forced it open wider than he'd wanted, allowing diagonal rain to wash into his still sleepy face. There, standing in front of him, illuminated by a blaze of lightning, stood a tall, shrouded figure, a dark cloak flapping around her. The figure stared back at him, breathing deeply, an unusual hungry fire in her many eyes.

CHAPTER 3

The plan unveils....

The figure pulled back the cowl of the soaked black cloak, exposing ten blinking eyes. Jimmy noticed the small piece of visible skin on her face was grazed and looked painful. The eye above the skinned portion, and the ones on top of her head, were heavily bloodshot, weeping thick, yellow ooze.

"Madam Shrill?" he said.

She removed one hand from whatever she clutched beneath her cloak and wiped her eyes. "Jimmy," she said, breathing heavily as she glanced over her left shoulder.

"Madam Shrill, please come in out of the rain," Jimmy said, opening the door the rest of the way.

Madam Shrill's eyes narrowed, her expression hardening as she said, "Jimmy, there's little time. They have found me. I'd hoped to have more time with you, but—"

"What do you mean? Who found you?"

"Jimmy, listen to me. I'm in grave danger!" she snapped, pulling the cloak tighter around her shivering body. "It's been four years since you found the *Elixir of Light*, but it's also been four years since Professor Tinker disappeared. He came to my library the night before he was to take you on that field trip to meet the ghoul contacts, the day you met Mr Gibbs, the Watchmaker. He wouldn't tell me all the details, but he did mention a plot to destroy the elders by someone close to us … a friend. He told me he had to find out the truth, but he was never seen again.

"Jimmy, I figured it out. I know who's behind the plan to destroy everything. It's not who you think. There will be no healing of the earth, or a rebirth. Everything will be destroyed. Every human soul will be cast as a prisoner for eternity. Jimmy, we must stop him. He will do terrible things to this world."

Lightning tore through the night sky as the howls of the bloodhounds drew closer. Madam Shrill began to pant as she turned to look at the entrance to the Close. "They're here! They've found me! I must go now, but I want you to take this." She reached under her cloak and pulled out a thick, leather-bound book.

Jimmy's arm jerked under the weight of the book.

"Jimmy, I need to tell you the truth, but I can't, not here. Meet me tomorrow at nine o'clock." She passed him a small, folded note. Before he could reply, she turned and shuffled to the silver gate. When she looked back at him, her many eyes were filled with sadness and fear. "There's a dark storm approaching, and you are at the centre of it."

"Jimmy!" a familiar voice shouted from behind him at the top of the stairs. "Who's at the door at this hour?"

Before Jimmy could reply, the gate slammed shut. He stepped out into the downpour in his bare feet and waded into a puddle, but Madam Shrill was already gone, the Close empty. He walked back inside and closed the door behind him. Above him, his mother stared down from the landing, illuminated by the light over her head.

So much had changed in the past four years. He hadn't been able to leave the castle much to visit, but he'd noticed a notable difference as soon as he stepped into the house. It had caught him by surprise. The only way he could think to explain it was if he'd walked out of a house in the morning, expecting the harsh reality of a bitter winter, but instead found a warm, gentle breeze carrying the tantalising aroma of roses, with the sound of skylarks singing on the wind. The house, and in fact his mother, just seemed different.

She had lost a considerable amount of weight, and her voice was softer, gentler, after she'd stopped smoking. Her new clothes and hairstyle gave her a confidence that Jimmy had never seen before. But he could see it in her eyes; every time Marjorie looked at him, or held him, he could see the sadness and regret there. But she was trying to make amends for the past. But maybe more importantly, changing for the future.

"Jimmy?" Marjorie said inquisitively.

"It's okay, Mum. It was no one. As he wiped the excess water from the leather binding of the book, he read the title.

The Life of Huic Ostiarius

With a warm smile, Marjorie walked back into her bedroom. "Be careful, Jimmy," she said, then closed the bedroom door.

Tucking the heavy book under his arm, Jimmy walked up the stairs to his own bedroom. The fifth and tenth steps creaked as soon as he put pressure on them. When he reached the landing, he looked through a gap in his mother's door. A sliver of the landing light cast a thin yellow beam that highlighted a picture on the table. A picture of Bill Threepwood, his father. Jimmy remembered his dream as the words rolled around in his head.

'I've tried everything to escape, but I'm lost. There is no way out for me.'

Thinking about it for a few moments, Jimmy smiled and pulled the door shut.

CHAPTER 4

The history of life and death….

Easing his bedroom door shut, Jimmy turned on the light and scurried to his bed. The grand book bounced on the springs as he dropped it in the middle of it. Heart racing with anticipation, he knelt on the floor, curious about what the book contained. *Who was Huic Ostiarius? An elder? What if it's Lord Trident's real name … or maybe the man charged with keeping Tyranacus locked at the centre of the earth?*

The cover creaked as he opened it. As he cast his eyes over the words, **Chapter One**, a freak wind bounced off his window, startling Jimmy. He could almost feel it bow under the pressure. The bedroom light sizzled and crackled before going out, then briefly struggled back on for a moment before the room was cast into darkness.

Jimmy pushed himself up and walked to the light switch. Staring at the light, as though willing the bulb to re-ignite, he flicked the plastic switch, on, off, on, off, but nothing.

Sighing, he walked back to the bed, knelt down and clicked his right fingers. His hand was immediately engulfed in a roaring green flame. Staring at the page, he was slightly startled by the image of a small boy, who Jimmy guessed must have been about twelve, staring back intently with his raven black locks flowing in an invisible wind. Pausing for a moment, Jimmy shook his head, feeling sure the image hadn't been on the page when he first looked. A creepy grin spread across the boy's face as he rubbed his hands together, and his vibrant emerald eyes sparkled to life.

Staring intently at the boy, Jimmy ran his fingers over the page. He could almost feel it sucking the moisture into the paper. A glimmer of green, almost a black aura, flickered behind the boy, casting a dark shadow across his face. Jimmy could see something behind his eyes, an evil presence lurking in the glooms. The tint of green reflected off his elegant, pearl-white gown which covered him from head to toe. Circling the neckline and trailing down the centre, almost like buttons, was a golden, silk-like pattern that seemed to emphasise power and stature.

The boy smiled again, sending a wave of unease through Jimmy, like unseen fingers stroking the back of his neck, causing him to shudder. Mesmerised by the evil presence behind his eyes, Jimmy lifted his left fingers. His skin pulled for a second, as though it had bonded with the page. He pulled more firmly, and his fingers were finally released.

Looking back, he saw the boy had aged by at least ten years, the shadow of whiskers noticeable on his prominent jawline. He had grown to at least six feet, but the sinister presence behind his eyes was still clearly visible. Jimmy could only describe it as the shrivelled embodiment of evil, covered in a cloak of fresh, vibrant skin.

The howling winds surged past Jimmy's house, gently nudging the foundations. The page rippled gently as the young man's head burst into flames, and a thousand screams vibrated inside Jimmy's mind. The green flame on his hand faded as a fiery skull erupted from the page. Like a screaming banshee, it travelled straight through him before it faded into the air. Jimmy staggered, grabbing his chest, feeling as though a thick, black tar was devouring his internal organs. Coughing and spluttering, awareness returned to his mind, and he snapped awake from wherever he had just been.

Eyes watering, his mouth felt and tasted like sand, but his hand was still alight. When the page suddenly turned, the house lights pinged back on. Jimmy found the following page blank. As he stared at the blank page, a small black box gradually materialized in the middle portion of the paper. The background became dusty grey with a white cross in the centre. In the bottom right-hand corner sat a small grey 'play button' symbol and a timer—20:05. The layout of the square reminded Jimmy of a modern-day internet video feed.

Poking the play button with his finger, the square came alive, radiating a silver light as a countdown spread across the page from five to one, each one highlighted by a beep and the distinct crackle of an old film. When the page reached one, Jimmy heard a loud 'click' from behind him, and the sound of a reel turning slowly on an old projector. As the silver video burst to life, an image was cast through Jimmy's body, taking over his room.

Inside the projection now, Jimmy could feel the warmth radiating from the wall next to him. Though dark inside the scene, he sensed he stood in a large cave, or cavern, and his feet were on a steep, stone staircase. Bending down, he used his hands to feel at least five steps climbing upward.

Standing, his lower back bumped against a solid metal railing. He ran his left hand over the smooth surface, feeling heat generated from within. Reaching out past the railing, Jimmy found only empty air. Turning slowly while keeping a firm hold on the pulsing metal, he toed the steps, sending small fragments of crumbled dust over the edge.

The echo of approaching voices startled him and he crouched down, his foot flicking a loose pebble over the edge. His heartbeat quickened as the small stone clipped the surrounding walls, but he never heard it hit the bottom.

"Majordomo," a voice spluttered. "Please illuminate the fires."

Out of the shadows came a tall, spindly man with short hazel hair, wearing a green version of the boy's gown from the book. As he climbed the steps towards him, Jimmy crawled backwards like a crab, hitting his head on the railings, but the man completely ignored him. Thrusting his hand forward, Jimmy swiped at the man's body, but it went straight through him.

He can't see me, Jimmy thought as he dragged himself to his feet. He reached forward again and pushed his hands into the man's chest. They flickered grey, and he could see particles of dust in the light, as though he had placed them in front of the lens of an unseen projector.

Confident he couldn't be seen, Jimmy studied the man as he passed the lower steps, his flowing emerald gown swinging behind him. Jimmy recognised certain mannerisms, the way he held his posture, his movement. Climbing the stairs, he stepped closer and studied the man's face. "Majordomo? Is that that really you?" he whispered to himself. The man's skin was as soft as silk with perfect chiselled features that radiated life. Puzzled, Jimmy murmured, "What happened to you?"

*

"Majordomo, please illuminate the fires."

Majordomo reached into the pocket of his fine robes and pulled out a handful of purple sand. With his firm gaze locked on the blackness ahead, he allowed some of the fine grains to filter through the gaps between his fingers back into the pocket. When only a few grains remained, he stepped closer to the railing.

"Yes, Master Trident," he replied, his voice youthful and teetering on the edge of excitement. Clenching his hand into a fist, he tossed the sand over the edge, then stepped back and watched.

Jimmy watched with him as the sand flittered into the air and disappeared into the darkness. Seconds passed, then a grumbling of rage stirred in the void far below, leaving the sweet aroma of flowers and wet rain in the cave. Jimmy leaned over the railing, seeing the distorted air below, reminding him of gas fumes.

The groaning became louder, more aggressive, as a vibration rumbled through the metal railing. Before Jimmy could react, the cavern was illuminated by an explosion of purple fire.

CHAPTER 5

The Council of Elders….

The fire continued to roar, maintaining a constant level parallel to the top of the stone staircase high above Jimmy. Looking upward, he could see the stone stairs led to a platform of some kind. Below him, the staircase dropped about thirty steps before turning a sharp ninety-degree angle, then continuing down another thirty steps, leading into a dimly lit room.

Fear caused his stomach to churn as Jimmy looked over the railing into the bottomless pit. The flickering flame and tint of purple light showed the spectacular cavern in all its glory. The walls were covered in a layer of glistening gold, and lodged within them sat countless jewels spanning all the colours of the rainbow. Awed by the sight, Jimmy's mouth dropped open.

He could see now that the railing he held onto was also made from gold. It kept people from falling over the edge into the endless pit of flames below.

"My Masters," Majordomo shouted. "The fire has been ignited and the passage to the Vantage Room is clear." He stood in the middle of the steps, bowed, and remained focused on the floor.

"Good," a familiar voice shouted from within the dimly lit room.

A lone man, filled with confidence and self-importance, almost glided from within the doorway. As his foot touched the first step a boom of footsteps stomped in unison from behind him.

Boom, Boom, Che. Boom, Boom, Che, rang in the air like a drum. A light tingle tickled across Jimmy's body as the voices matched the beat of the standing march.

*"**Aventor!**" Boom, Boom, Che. "**Aventor!**" Boom, Boom, Che. "**Aventor**...!"*

The lone man climbed the steps, his unkempt brown moustache covering the lower part of his face. His remaining brown hair flapped at the sides as he walked. The man approached the servant, Majordomo, who dropped down on one knee and held out his left hand for Lord Trident to touch.

Grasping his outstretched hand, Lord Trident gripped it firmly as six other men and two women draped in long white robes marched up the steps to stand beside them, constantly repeating the ritual song.

Trident looked down at Majordomo, and through the bristles of his brown moustache said, "Argh, the second of my creations. The creature I shall spread across this new world, this ... Earth. My first design wasn't quite right." He smiled. "Too many eyes, though I have the perfect role for her. But you ... you are perfect. This world will form from your DNA, but I will need you to remain here as my servant."

"Yes, my Master," Majordomo replied.

The other eight council members channelled either side of Trident and Majordomo, where they continued to the top to form a guard of honour.

"Come, my son, lead me to the Rose Door and the creation of this world."

Majordomo pushed to his feet and walked ahead of Trident under the raised arms of the other elders. As he passed them, he looked at each of their faces. Some he had seen about the castle, but they had been too busy to talk to a mere servant. Others, he knew well. Majordomo could hear his master's footsteps closing behind and didn't dare slow down, but as he passed Aralynn to his left, he offered her a wink and a smile. Her smooth, lavender skin glowed against the backdrop of the golden walls. He could smell her fresh curly hair which tumbled down her back and across her face. Her yellow eyes glowed like distant stars.

Looking at Lorratt Del-Vargo on his right, he bowed in admiration. Majordomo felt unworthy to be walking past one of the greatest chemists ever. He had spent months watching Lorratt making the most fascinating potions. Inspired, he'd tried to make his own, but each effort had failed miserably. He just didn't have the magic touch. As he flicked his thick black hair to the side, Lorratt returned the smile and the nod.

The next male in the line didn't smile as he stared at Majordomo. A giant of a man, Roland Perrier stroked the fine bristles growing on his face. Majordomo noticed the gentle shade of grey slowly taking hold in the beard. His round belly stuck out in front of him, clearly visible under the woven gown. With his arms crossed over his belly, Majordomo could see the thickness of his fingers on his ogre hands, thick patches of hair engulfing various areas like a miniature forest.

Reaching the top of the stairs, he approached the last of the elders, the youngest of the council by a number of years. His piercing emerald eyes and jet-black hair made him stand out against the others. Intimidated, Majordomo felt there was something not quite right with his eyes or smile, but he couldn't put his finger on what. As he passed Huic Ostiarius, he could almost feel an invisible presence surrounding him, leaking through his aura like a heavy dark cloud, pulling at

Majordomo, and he quickly looked away. Reaching the top of the stairs, he walked along the narrow platform.

Majordomo stopped when Lord Trident coughed. He rested against the railing as Lord Trident stepped in front of a giant stone door. He stared in wonder at the rough, harsh surface, but engraved within was the most beautiful object he had ever seen. The rose, as he had heard it called, was perfectly carved from stem to blossom. So fixed was he on the rose, Majordomo barely noticed the other elders leave their formation and stand in two rows behind Lord Trident. He heard a distant voice echo through the cavern as a sweet aroma filled his nose and warmed his chest.

"Goooo now…."

"Majordomo!" a voice said acidly, snapping him out of his dreamlike state. "Your job here is done. You may go and attend your duties."

Disappointed, Majordomo wanted to see what lay behind the door. To see how this … world would be created. Inhaling sharply, he stared down at the floor. "Yes, Master."

He bowed once more and walked back through the two rows of elders, back down the stone steps. Reaching the point where he had cast the grains of sand into the void, he stopped and looked discretely back over his shoulder just in time to see the rose carving illuminate. The vibrant green stem bled upward, igniting the magnificent red petals, once again flooding the air with its sweet fragrance, followed by an almighty scraping of stone on stone as the door opened, and the elders disappeared inside.

CHAPTER 6

The Rose Door….

Absorbed in the movie, Jimmy continued to watch as Majordomo walked dejectedly back down the stone stairs and out of view. Turning back to face the glowing red rose, he tingled with growing excitement. A cloud of dust filled the air as the door scraped open. Jimmy ran up the steps as Lord Trident led the elders into the room, his footsteps not making a sound. He stood at the doorway and watched.

As the dust settled, he could see a small, rectangular path of light illuminate the dark shadows of the room. It came from the fire in the cavern from behind him. Lord Trident walked to the edge of the light. As the tips of his toes became lost in the blackness, a thin green vine slithered across the floor and coiled up Trident's leg to his waist and began to squeeze.

Huic panicked and broke formation, running to his aid.

"No, Huic!" shouted Trident. "Don't move."

Before Huic could take another step, two more vines whipped into view from beyond the gloom and latched around his wrists. As he struggled, thorns burst through the fibres of the vines, shredding Huic's sleeves before digging deep into his skin. Huic groaned in pain and tried to move as more thorny vines wrapped around his ankles and squeezed.

"Stop, my precious," Trident commanded as he stroked the vines coiled around his body. "It's okay. He's not here to steal the pen. He's here merely to help facilitate its magic."

A deep routed murmur roared from within the blackness as the prickles released their grip on Huic and unravelled, sliding back into the shadows. Clapping his hands, Trident filled the room with light.

The other elders stared in wonder, but Jimmy's focus remained on the raven-haired boy who stood in the middle of the room. His face looked like thunder as he scratched at the many cuts on his wrists. Huic's eyes turned black with anger as he stared at the bushes and leaves scattered with pink, red and yellow buds spread across the room.

"I hope you're okay, Huic," Trident said. "I thought this would be a wonderful defence to protect the pen from intruders. This…" He gestured with his arm at the giant entanglement of vines and leaves at the back of the room. "…is the Genus Rosa, or you may prefer to call it, a rose. The giant plant groaned and fidgeted, unravelling its leaves, sending a gentle ripple through the bushes on either side of the room.

Jimmy turned his attention from Huic to study the room. He could feel a gentle mist of water against his face. The room itself was glistening white, almost sterile, as though no one had ever stepped foot in it before. Reaching over the threshold, he touched the floor with his hands. It felt cold and smooth, with the same texture as marble. It squeaked as he ran his fingers across it.

In the middle of the room were three small white steps that led up to a platform. The platform was empty apart from a waist-high wooden table with a large rectangular glass case sat across the top. Narrowing his eyes, Jimmy could see something in the middle, but he was too far away to see what.

He stepped into the room, his feet slipping on the smooth, almost icy, surface. Regaining his balance, Jimmy took slower steps as he walked around the elders, who had congregated in front of the steps. Trident walked up the steps and stood behind the glass case, holding his hands high in the air.

Suddenly the room fell deathly silent. The eight elders and Jimmy hung on Trident's every word.

"Today, my friends, will mark the beginning. A new world … a perfect world, will rise from the ashes of our fallen home, Nola. This world, this Earth, will grow with vigour and beauty. It will be populated with the creatures of our creation."

Jimmy looked in the glass case, finding a long, elegant green stem leading to a magnificent red rose with luscious, vibrant petals. The end of the stem became the golden tip of a quill pen. The delicate pen was lying flat, held in place by two carved wooden holders.

"My friends," Trident continued as he lifted the glass case and gently placed it on the floor beside him. "This is the time to prosper, the time of life … and it is all given by this, the most perfect creation of them all … the Rose Pen." He lifted it high above his head.

The room erupted with the ritual chant, "*Aventor! Aventor!*" followed by the stomping of feet to the beat of *Boom, Boom, Che. Boom, Boom, Che….*

Through a cacophony of cheers, his hands trembling from excitement, Trident took hold of the pen and marched down the steps. He walked past the elders and out of the room, barely able to contain his joy.

Jimmy followed Trident and the elders towards the door. Hearing the grumble of the giant plant in the shadows of the room, he stopped at the entrance to look back. Before he could react, four thorny vines flew through the air towards him. He flinched as they slammed straight through his ghostly body, hitting the floor on the other side. Sensing his presence, the tips of the vines moved like snakes as they felt around the floor, but they couldn't find him and eventually recoiled.

Jimmy gave a long, deep sigh of relief as he hurriedly slipped out onto the landing, the door grinding shut behind him.

He followed the gentle fragrance of rose through the narrow passage being illuminated by the blazing purple fire. He caught up just as the last two elders approached another stone door.

The female in front, with brown curly hair tumbling down her back, turned to Huic. In a soft and caring voice, she said, "It will be okay, Huic. Lord Trident has told us the key to enter this room. You just need to think of Lord Trident."

"But what if we think of something else?" the raven-haired boy replied inquisitively.

With a radiating smile, she replied, "I don't think you want to know. Let's just say the thought is like a password, and I won't be forgetting it." She disappeared through the door.

Huic turned to look over his shoulder towards where Jimmy stood. A snarl spread across his face as he rubbed his fingers over the cuts on his wrists.

Jimmy gasped, clutching at the crushing pain in his chest. He could feel a blackness coursing through his veins. Breathing rapidly, his vision blurred, and he staggered back, holding onto the railing. When he looked up, he saw Huic's angry gaze hadn't shifted from the Rose Door. With a swirl of his gown, Huic disappeared into the second room. Instantly, calm returned to Jimmy's body. Taking a deep breath, he too thought of Lord Trident and took the plunge of faith into the room.

Landing, Jimmy panicked, feeling as though the air had been sucked from his lungs. It took a moment to catch his breath. A fresh breeze swirled around his body, the air different here, cleaner. As it filled his lungs, it seemed to rejuvenate his body.

As he took in his surroundings, Jimmy felt a fluffy white cloud crash into his shins, separating before it drifted aimlessly around him. The floor was a perfect, clear blue sky. Looking down, he saw he was at the highest point of the castle, a moat with flowing, crystal-clear water far below. *That's the black sea,* he thought with disbelief. *What happened to thick black tar with floating white spirits?*

Jimmy's gaze was diverted to a spluttering and coughing Lord Trident. Glancing up, he saw where the sky floor led to a further set of white steps leading up to a grand circular platform. Sitting in a circle on top of the platform, in nine egg-shaped white seats, were the elders. In the most prominent seat, directly in front of Jimmy, almost like a throne, sat Lord Trident.

Huic sat to Trident's right, the second seat from the top. He was almost swallowed up by the chair, but sat there looking around confidently, watching the other elders.

"Council members, arise!" Trident commanded. They all stood in unison.

The room started to gently hum, and for the first time, Jimmy noticed the saucer-shape of the glistening white room. Beyond the seats, he saw five rounded, stretched black windows spread evenly spaced across the back wall. The floor began to vibrate, and hydraulics hissed at the release of pressurised gas, and the saucer slowly started to rotate around them.

The saucer increased its speed, becoming faster and faster. The outside world became a blur of intertwined colours.

Holding his arms out to keep his balance, Jimmy saw Trident flail both his arms, as though leading a symphony.

"Elders, what do you think of the design for the sky?"

There was a collective mumbling but, smiling through a long white beard that rested far below the level of his chest, the old man sat to the left of Huic said. "My Lord, the colours are expressive and vibrant, and the … clouds, I believe you called them, have a number of roles. Not only are they aesthetically pleasing, but they—"

"Enough, Oler," Trident said, cutting him off. "A simple yes or no would have sufficed."

As though holding a wand, Trident thrust and swept the pen through the air. Jimmy recognised the outline of trees, birds, animals, mountains, and continents form before Trident cast them through the spinning carousel and out into the world.

Elephants, dragons, whales, were all drawn and unleashed through the windows. Trident, awash with power, looked like an artist scooping paint from his pallet and expressing himself with wave after wave of creation. The saucer spun and spun, churning out every colour, every creation, and then it stopped … and the madness slowed, and Lord Trident dropped to his knees in exhaustion, the tip of the pen scraping the floor.

Breathing frantically, his face alight in glory, Lord Trident looked through the windows at the colours spreading across the land, covering the haze of yellow and dull brown with vibrant greens for as far as the eye could see.

He dragged himself slowly to his feet amidst cheers and celebration. "It is done. The world will flourish and become the haven for life. It is ready, except for the primary species." Snapping a petal from the end of the flower pen, Trident breathed his DNA onto the petal and threw it high into the air.

It fluttered before being sucked out through the centre black window.

Beaming, he bowed his head, and Jimmy heard Trident whisper, "Live, my new world, live…."

CHAPTER 7

The untimely death….

Deep in the back of Jimmy's mind, like a distant, hollow echo, he could hear the continuous clicking and clanking of the reel turning. With one last loud 'click', his mind fell silent.

A gentle gust of wind circled in Jimmy's bedroom, scooping a folded piece of paper from the top of the chest of drawers before launching it high into the air. As the paper glided down, the edges of the sheet flapped like a small bird before it nose-dived and crashed pointy-tip first into Jimmy's face.

Jerking awake, he slapped his hand over the burning sensation on his right cheek. He looked around, expecting to still be in the Vantage Room having an audience with Lord Trident and the elders. Instead, he was back in his little bedroom, sunlight seeping beneath the closed curtains. He rubbed at his eyes as the memory of the night before flooded back. Lord Trident, the elders, the Rose Pen, and the spinning room. As Jimmy slumped against the wall, the small piece of paper on his lap flipped over, catching his attention. *Madam Shrill*, he thought in a panic.

Unravelling the note, the words came into view in big black letters.

**Tomorrow, nine o'clock, Black Friars Alley.
You know where it is.**

Jimmy sat staring at the note for a moment, his mind spinning. Out of the corner of his eye, he saw the little grey clock on his dresser. **8:50 am.**

"Madam Shrill!" he shouted, scrambling to his feet. He moved towards the bedroom door, then ran back again to grab a coat. Scrubbing his hands over his face, he ran out of his bedroom, down the stairs and out the door. As the door closed, the lion-head knocker banged hard against its metal body, but Jimmy was already gone, halfway down the street.

He heard the village clock strike nine as he ran through the small local shops. He knew he was still a few minutes away and picked up the pace.

As he turned past a solid stone wall into a narrow alleyway, a blast of wild energy shot through his body, stopping Jimmy dead in his tracks. Sensing a presence, he looked all around but found no one there. He was alone. Above him, a white street sign with thick black letters was stuck to a wall.

Black Friars Alley

Jimmy ran again, flying past a variety of smaller shops, then under an archway. Without thought, he slammed his hand down on a small, waist-high metal post in the shape of an owl and pulled to help add momentum. Bursting into a church courtyard, he caught the scent of freshly cut grass. He slowed as the path opened ahead of him, then stopped to survey the scene.

He had to do a double take when he caught sight of Madam Shrill. She sat to his right in the far corner, resting on the centre of three giant boulders. Jimmy smiled, but he was too far away to see Madam Shrill's face. He walked slowly towards her, his smile fading when she didn't move.

Something was terribly wrong here. Jimmy picked up his pace when he noticed Madam Shrill was slouched over. "Madam Shrill!" he said, trying to help her stand.

Madam Shrill murmured, and Jimmy could feel moisture on his hand. Pulling it away, he found it stained with thick red blood. He looked down, beginning to tremble when he noticed blood all over the stones. As she dropped down to her knees, a yellow-handled knife fell to the floor, clattering on the gravelled path.

"Madam Shrill!"

Slowly and weakly, she raised all her eyes to stare up at Jimmy, regret visible in her expression. In great pain, she coughed, and half of her eyes closed. With the last of her strength, she whispered, "Jimmy, the bird of ... impending disast ... er—" Her body twitched, and her remaining eyes closed for the last time.

CHAPTER 8

Reuniting the Spectres of the Past....

Ahaze of swirling, blustery wind blew through the entrance of the quaint village. Fine grains of sand pelted the thirty-mile-an-hour speed and welcome signs on either side of the road.

Welcome to Perrygrove. Please drive carefully

The sheer magnitude and power of the storm corroded the thin metal signs, ravaging them. They became shrivelled and disfigured before all three signs collapsed in a pile of rust on the side of the road.

Alarmed, the shopkeepers could only watch as the cyclone devoured their village. At the heart of the storm, a distorted black image flicked his wrist, controlling the powerful energy. One by one, doors slammed and bells jingled as the shopkeepers scurried back inside. Glass windows cracked and split under the sheer force, allowing sand to seep in through the gaps and pile up on the floors. As the haze moved slowly towards the forgotten clock tower perched on the centre of a tiny roundabout, the distinct smell of salt filled the air.

Bewildered shopkeepers peered out of their windows, watching as the storm stopped at the back of the clock tower. Tentacles spread out, twisting and turning, covering every inch of the stone frame. Slowly, the probing fingers disintegrated, and the storm faded away, leaving behind a solitary man who stared about intently.

Licking his cracked lips, Imjimn-Ra could feel his tight, leathery skin pull every time he used his facial muscles, but he could feel nothing when he touched the smooth, hard surface of his face. The nerve endings of his dark brown, swollen fingers had shrivelled and died long ago. Every one of his senses was numb. As his shredded mummy wrapping flapped in the breeze, his black eyes stared at the large crack split straight through the middle of the carved headless woman draped in a long black gown. The wreckage had opened a doorway leading down a spiralling staircase into blackness.

Stepping over the pile of rubble and stone, Imjimn-Ra groaned as he swiped aside the thick layer of cobwebs and descended the stone staircase.

His heavy foot echoed as he took one final step onto the stone-tiled floor into the small, damp room. Flames burst into life in the four corners. Radiant light bounced off the reflective surfaces of the treasure collected over a thousand years. Walking forward, his feet pushed aside gold plates, coins and ornaments, sending them clattering over the floor.

In the centre of the room, Imjimn-Ra looked through a glass case stood on top of a wooden stand. Narrowing his eyes, he could make out the title etched in the leather cover.

The Forgotten Past. The Diary of Eunice Aurabella

Anger swelled inside him as he thrust his right hand forward, removing the book before he slammed the glass case across the room. It shattered on the wall, raining glass onto the corner flame, where it flickered and crackled.

A plume of dust clouded his vision as he snapped open the book. Flipping frantically through the pages, he finally found what he was looking for. His eyes widened as he stared at it for a moment … remembering.

He tore the page from the book and kicked the stand. It toppled over, sending the book sprawling across the room. With a bounce, the spine snapped, sending the dirty brown pages spreading across the floor.

Stepping back into the sunlight, Imjimn-Ra walked with purpose to a church spire a short distance away. The years of neglect were clear to see. Images, memories, raced through his mind as he stared at the barely visible stone graves almost completely covered in grass and thick green moss. The church roof was in complete ruins. A slight breeze caused two tiles to slide off and shatter on the path below. Imjimn-Ra gritted his teeth as he marched into a small wooden shack masked by the shadow of an eerie black mountain.

A black cross was painted the length of the door. As it swung open and he stepped onto the wooden floorboards, the pungent smell of death and raw sewage swirled and prodded at his dead sense of smell.

When a floorboard creaked under foot, he kicked aside the four smashed stools. Imjimn-Ra bent down and picked up a green emerald stone on a chain and drooped it over his forearm. *Fool!* he thought with a snarl, discarding the stone onto the floor. *Enoh Stones. Did you really think that could stop the Children of Tyranacus?*

Imjimn-Ra's gaze followed the trail of dried green blood along the floor, up the wall, past savage claw marks in the wood, leading to a thick bluish-green stain on the ceiling. Shaking his head, he walked to the sink and pulled out the piece of paper he'd taken from the diary and placed it on the draining board.

He ran his fingers over the page, studying the last picture ever taken of the four of them together, the four of them before his companion, his friend, turned on him, turned on them. His finger rubbed slowly over Lady Aurabella. The corners of her mouth turned up as she stared into Vesty's eyes. "You fools," he whispered, reaching behind his back to pull out half a jagged flute from his waistband. Staring at the picture, he remembered how Vesty would never part with the instrument. He ran his finger over the sharp edge of the flute, then whispered, "You should have waited. You should have never tried to take them on alone. Even so young, so weak, they are still a threat. But rest easy, my friends, for I will avenge you. I have a plan ... a plan to divide and conquer. To pull them apart from within. They will destroy themselves ... with just a bit of help from an old friend."

Reaching out, he grabbed the rusted brown tap. It squealed, and the pipe clanked before eventually spitting out a few droplets of dirty brown water. Catching the drops on his fingertips, he carefully sprinkled tiny grains of sand over the droplets. As the sand absorbed into the moisture, he flicked it onto the floor.

A bone-chilling, pig-like squeal and hiss filled the room as a small black slug wriggled free, shedding its coat of water and sand. As it grew, slime absorbed from its body, soaking into the floorboards. The black slug morphed into a hideous, slime-covered young girl. The creature's skin was a dull grey, and its short-cropped, greasy black hair stuck to her face. Her empty black eyes stared back at her creator.

"You look perfect, my dear," Imjimn-Ra said. "My new creature to rip the children apart from the inside. You, the Garn, will follow my orders!"

A thick black slug flicked out of her mouth and twitched back and forth, squelching in its own slime. The slug morphed into a tongue, and words slithered out, "Yesss, the Garn will serve my new master."

The leather squeaked as a smile spread across Imjimn-Ra's face. "Then let's make you desirable." He stepped forward, placing his palm on her head.

The Garn jolted back as a storm of sand surged into her skin, absorbing the thick grey slime. As it filtered through her body, her hair changed to a golden blonde colour. It grew in length, nestling below her shoulders. Her eyes turned blue as the sea, her white skin silky as a feather. The sand clogged her pores, releasing an irresistible rosy pheromone.

"No man can resist you now!" he said as she twirled in her new red dress. "You will drive a wedge straight through the hearts of the Children of Tyranacus."

CHAPTER 9

Remorse....

Jimmy eased the back door shut, then planted his back against the glass panels and stared into space. His stomach churned and his legs threatened to give out on him. In his mind, he could still see Madam Shrill's blood on his hands, still see the splatter of dried blood on the stone. He felt lost.

What did she mean by 'The bird of impending disaster'?

His weakened legs finally gave out and he slid down the door to sit on the floor. "I don't know what it means?" he murmured. His mind spun, seeing flashes of Madam Shrill's face, the moment her eyes closed. "Black Friars," he whispered, pausing. "Why Black Friers?"

He closed his eyes, trying to calm his racing thoughts. *What happened out there? I remember being late. The chimes of the clock. I ran through the alley and saw Madam Shrill in the distance.* Jimmy frowned, concentrating. *Birds were twittering all around us, but something was off. I'm missing something.* His head began to pound, and pain bit into his right hand.

What did I do to my hand? What did I hit it on? There was nothing there?

Then it hit him, like a switch had been flicked on. There had been a small brown pole placed in the centre of the alley to keep cars from driving through. Retracing his steps in his mind, he recalled gripping the top of the metal pole to help his momentum. But why would that be important? Puzzled, he reached up to scratch the side of his head. His right foot twitched and he unintentionally kicked one of the wooden kitchen cupboards.

"Jimmy," a concerned voice shouted from the top of the stairs. "Is that you?"

Jimmy paused, cursing. All he wanted was to be left alone with his thoughts. The answers he needed were dangling right on the edge.

"Jimmy," a soft, caring voice whispered, "are you okay? Why are you sitting on the floor?"

Sighing, Jimmy looked up. "I'm okay, Mum. Just having a bit of a bad day, but I'm fine. Honestly."

"You don't look fine," she said, reaching out to help him stand. Marjorie kept hold of his arm while she rubbed his back. The muscles in his neck began to relax, and the pain in his head to ease.

"Why don't you go out and sit down in the living room, Jimmy. I'll put the kettle on. It'll make you feel better."

Jimmy paused, wondering what he should do.

"Go!" Marjorie said with stern authority, waving her hands at him.

Jimmy obeyed. He watched as Marjorie walked in a short time later carrying a teacup which rattled on the saucer. She smiled at Jimmy as she set it on the table next to him.

Jimmy noticed her eyes were filled with sorrow, but in the same instance, happiness. *Happiness because she'd been given a second chance to right her wrongs?* Warmth seeped into his fingers as he picked up the cup.

"I'm glad you decided to visit, Jimmy. It's been really nice seeing you." Her warm smile lit up the room. "I hope … I hope you can come a little more often."

An awkward silence followed. Jimmy didn't know how to answer. When the hairs stood up on his arms, he glanced around the room, his eyes coming to light on a picture that sat on the mantel. His father and mother just after they were married. *They looked so happy,* he thought, shifting his attention back to Marjorie. Returning her smile, he nodded. "I will. I promise."

"I wondered if later maybe you would fancy having a go at painting your room. We could go and pick out some colours. What do you think?"

Before he could reply, a dim, flashing red light covered the room, followed instantly by a high-pitched, wailing alarm. The red light in the living room faded, drifting into the kitchen. Jimmy put down his cup, some of the liquid spilling on the table. He followed the red light through the kitchen, up the stairs and into his bedroom. Opening the door, he found the book of Huic Ostiarius bouncing on the bed, the pages glowing.

As if sensing Jimmy's presence in the room, the leather binding flapped open, projecting a light over Jimmy, and the movie reel clicked into action. His bedroom melted away, and he once again stood as an apparition, an onlooker, outside the perfectly carved Rose Door.

A feeling of dread hit him almost immediately. The golden walls of the cavern pulsated red from the flashing lights, like a beating heart. The distant echo of an alarm screamed in time with his rapid breathing.

The Rose Door grinded open, and out rushed Lord Trident, panic plastered across his face. He was followed by the other eight elders, all still wearing their flowing white gowns. Startled, Jimmy stepped back, hitting his lower back on the railing. Feeling a vibration, he glanced over his shoulder into the bottomless pit.

Without pause, Trident and the elders filed into the Vantage Room. Jimmy followed. He remembered the clean air of before inside the room, the soft, fluffy clouds tickling the hairs on his legs as they drifted past. But unlike then, a great heat weighed him down this time, his sweat evaporating almost immediately. The occupants darted around, acting panicked.

Jimmy's heart began to race. Something bad had happened here. But what?

CHAPTER 10

The end of time….

Jimmy couldn't turn his gaze from the blood-red sky floor beneath his feet; the ominous clouds heavy and black instead of a fluffy white. Water swished around his boots. In the distance below, the once luscious green fields were now brown and yellow, dead. He hardly recognised the castle grounds. A breeze swept through the air, scooping up a ball of the lifeless soil and sweeping it along the wasteland, reminiscent of a sandstorm swirling across the Sahara Desert.

One of the panicked elders caught his attention, drawing his gaze towards a window in the saucer-shaped room. Lightning cracked, tearing open the earth's atmosphere, leaving a dark hole in space. A vacuum began to slowly suck what was left of life from the earth through the jagged hole. Drawn to the rectangular window, Jimmy stared in disbelief. Moisture had formed on the glass, and he wiped it away with his sleeve. He could barely breathe as he realized the sheer magnitude of the tear in space. It ran vertically from the sky to the ground. Even worse, he could see where other, much smaller tears, were beginning to form around it.

"What have they done!" Lord Trident shouted.

Jimmy turned to look, finding Lord Trident swishing the Rose Pen about in the air like a wand.

*

"What shall we do? What shall we do? No, I can fix this … the pen." Trident stared out into the world, horrified.

"No!" shouted Huic defiantly. "You are a fool! These creatures you love so much. Look … look at what they have done to your precious Earth! Two thousand years and look what they've done with it. They need to be punished, not rewarded! If you fix the damage, they will simply destroy it again!"

Lord Trident's shoulders drooped as he stared across the land, the weight of leadership slowly crushing his spirit. "What have they done?" he murmured. The world in front of him had been split apart and burned. Feeling his authority leaking away, he turned to face Huic, seeing only rage in the elder's eyes. But Trident didn't feel anger, only sorrow, because he knew Huic was right. He couldn't save them this time. His precious humans had recklessly destroyed his gift to them, a gift forged from his own hands after Nola had been destroyed. And how did they repay him? By destroying his world.

"What are you waiting for," shouted Huic, undermining Lord Trident by challenging him. "Destroy this world and lock them all in a prison in the planet's core to suffer for an eternity! They should have cared for the gifts we bestowed upon them."

In that moment, Lord Trident knew what had to be done. They couldn't look after his precious world. In their search for technology and power, they had brought it to the brink of disaster. Snapping his attention back to the elders, he shouted, "Silence!" to Huic. "How dare you challenge me. Try to tell me how to lead my people!" Trident clenched his fist, followed by the crunch and crackle of bones as an invisible band squeezed tight around Huic's chest.

Moaning in agony, Huic whispered, "I'm sorry, my Lord."

Trident released his grip, and Huic collapsed to his knees, holding his ribs and breathing heavily.

With his mind now clear, Lord Trident was determined to follow through with his plan. "My fellow elders. I must admit, Huic does have a point. This is not acceptable, and the humans must be punished for what they've done. They treat my gift as garbage and have demonstrated they cannot properly look after this world, but I can't just throw it away. They will be punished for what they've done here, and they will learn!"

Lord Trident looked out at the elders, staring each one in the eyes. "I will need three willing volunteers."

Confused, the other seven elders all looked at each other.

One hand slowly raised, belonging to a long, spindly body. "But, my Lord," Lorratt Del-Vargo said, "volunteer for what?"

His expression unreadable, Trident replied, "I will use some of your power to create the ultimate weapon. A beast that will control the very elements of the earth. A beast to wipe the planet clean. Once the deed is done, I will use the Rose Pen to heal the earth, and slowly, over time, life will begin again."

As gasps filled the air, Aralynn lunged forward, her soft hands held aloft. "No, my Lord, please. There must be another way. There must."

"No!" Trident shouted, his voice hard and firm. "There is no other way! They must learn from what they have done. Every two thousand years, the beast will rise, and the earth will be healed."

Tears trickled down Aralynn's cheeks. "But, my Lord, you love this earth. You love these people. Please don't do this."

With a long, deep sigh, Trident murmured, "They must learn."

CHAPTER 11

The forging of the beast….

Jimmy stared on in disbelief, stunned by Lord Trident's decision. His attention kept being drawn towards the window at the swirling carnage outside.

Huic slowly, painfully, clambered to his feet. The projector casting the world around him flickered and crackled, draining the colour, replacing his surroundings with a dull, empty greyness. The sound faded for a split second before the reel crunched and clicked, and the images flickered back to colour.

Jimmy watched as the eight elders all stared at the floor, doing their best to avoid eye contact with Lord Trident.

"If I do not get volunteers, I will be forced to choose three of you myself. It is your decision."

The elders glanced sideways at each other, several nodding while trying to keep their focus away from Trident. After a short pause, two elders stepped forward and walked up the stone staircase. Jimmy hadn't really paid any attention to these two before. They must have been standing towards the back of the group.

"Argh, Reginald Simkin," Lord Trident said as a small dwarf of a man climbed the steps and bowed. A black, meticulously groomed triangular beard spread from his jaw, but only a few strands of fine black hair remained on his shiny pate.

"And Rosaland Fellaini. I suspected it might be you two who would volunteer to give up your power to protect what is right."

Jimmy studied Rosaland's azure eyes as she nervously twisted the ends of her straight, shoulder-length blonde hair. The only blemish on her perfectly sculptured oval face was a deep scar running from her right eye to her cheek. A gentle breath left Jimmy's lips as she glided effortlessly across the floor, her thin figure still curvaceous.

"My Lord," asked Simkin, his voice gritty, "how much of our power will you take?"

"Do not worry, my old friend. You will have enough to remain on the council, but it will be diminished. As a reward for your bravery, I shall look after you and ensure your place in the new world."

Trident's eyes turned dark as he looked towards the rest of the group. "I still need one more volunteer?" he said, his tone acid.

From the back of the group, Huic Ostiarius pushed his way through, still nursing his ribcage. He held up his hand as he spoke, wincing in pain, "I will volunteer, my Lord. I will relinquish my power to destroy this world."

The dripping, blood-red floor turned black as Trident's mood rapidly deteriorated. His fist began to shake as he crushed it into a ball. "You would love to destroy this world, wouldn't you? You are a fool, Huic. I'm not going to destroy the world. I'm going to rebuild it to ensure it survives forever."

The tension in the room swelled as Huic cowered before Trident's angry gaze. Before Trident had a chance to enact any punishment, Oler Roindx stepped forward, his old feet dragging slowly across the floor. As he reached Trident, his spine crunched and moaned when he straightened his crooked back.

"Master, my body is old and frail. I have no use for the power within me. I renounce it to save this world." He bowed his head, yet kept his gaze focused on Huic."

Trident's frown softened as the frail old man stood next to the other two volunteers. As he held the Rose Pen aloft, Rosaland started to shake, closing her eyes.

Simkin reached out and wrapped his warm hands around hers. "It'll be okay," he whispered, giving the faintest hint of a smile.

With Trident's mood improved, Jimmy watched as the blackness in the floor returned to the blood-red colour of the sky outside. The petals on the Rose Pen opened, as though the first light of summer had seeped into the room. The golden pen glowed as Trident stepped to each of the willing volunteers and gently touched the tip of the fountain pen to their foreheads.

The room was suddenly cast into darkness. Jimmy could feel the gentle tremor in the walls as the projection once again rippled, sending cracked white lines before his eyes.

Then the room fell silent, filled only with a gentle hum.

The humming slowly became louder as three glowing orbs emerged from the chests of the three volunteers. As the orbs pulled clear, Jimmy could see the elders' bodies trying desperately to fight back and hold on. With a final forceful pull, the three orbs broke free and spun in the air around Trident's head.

One by one, starting with the frail Oler Roindex, the exhausted volunteers collapsed to the floor.

The orbs spun faster and faster, each filling the room with a vile ghostly scream, and showing a distorted image of a monstrous, fiery-red beast raging over the dying earth.

As the orbs spun around Trident's head, he thrust his hands forward, and the five windows in the saucer-shaped room exploded outward, filling the air with a burst of shattered glass. The three orbs flew out into the madness and crashed beyond the wooden drawbridge to the wasteland below. Smoke floated up from the three fiery craters they created.

Gasping for air, Trident said, "Come, my elders. Come and see the creature that will change the dynamics of this world forever. I want us to have front-row seats for the changing of the world."

A thick yellow smog filtered in through the open windows, soiling the clean air with the scent of brimstone and magma.

Crouching on the floor, the three volunteers tried to lift their heads, but they could barely find the energy to open their eyes.

"It's okay, my friends, it has worked," Lord Trident said. "The creature has been forged. Rest now, saviours of this world. You deserve it. We will go watch this momentous occasion and then return for you." Signalling with his hands, he sent Aralynn, Roland Perrier and Lorratt Del-Vargo to help the three fallen elders to their egg-shaped seats. The comfort of the chairs squeezed around their bodies like a glove, and their heads slumped forward to rest on the table.

Jimmy started to follow Lord Trident and the others elders as they marched out of the room. Everyone except Huic Ostiarius. Jimmy stopped to watch as Huic, holding his damaged ribs, walked back to the three volunteers slumped in their chairs. He gently rubbed Oler Roindex's fine white hair, the old man barely conscious. "Thank you," he whispered. "I don't think I could have taken much more of Lord Trident's punishment. I won't forget this act of kindness, but mark my words, Lord Trident's reign is coming to an end."

CHAPTER 12

The Beast has been released….

Jimmy's feet clanked over the wooden slats of the drawbridge, knowing none of the elders would hear his ghostly form. He stood next to the hulking frame of Roland Perrier and watched as a faint trickle of light shone from the centre of the three small circular craters. The lights intensified, then slowly merged, forming a glowing triangle. The ground started to shake, and a crimson hand burst through the earth. With an almighty squeal, the long black nails protruding through the tips of its fingers thrashed right before a second hand smashed through.

"Master," Aralynn whispered, "shouldn't we be prepared. What if it attacks us?"

"Nonsense," Trident roared. "The beast is forged from the souls of the elders. It will know its master. But…" He rubbed his chin. "…maybe we should afford ourselves a barrier against the elements."

Turning back to Sepura Castle, he repeatedly moved the Rose Pen in a giant circle, and a yellow, domed-shaped bubble formed around them. When Lord Trident stopped, the misty bubble hardened, creating a transparent, rock-hard shell.

Lorratt Del-Vargo tapped his knuckle on the giant dome, the echoing clank spreading out into the distance beyond the castle.

With an almighty roar, the red beast dragged itself from the earth and stood snarling at the group of onlookers, thick slivers of saliva dripping from its enormous fangs. Its blood-red skin stretched over its huge rippling muscles, and its glittering obsidian eyes were filled with an unholy rage. In the centre of its head erupted a single, thick, jet-black horn, similar to a rhinoceros, a symbol of pure power, strength and fury.

Snarling, the beast reached behind its back and yanked out a glistening black axe. Holding it aloft, the heavens crackled and groaned under the beast's control. Whips of lightning ripped through the air and exploded into the blade, channelling its entire wrath into the monster. As the charge drained, the beast, the embodiment of evil, held its arms out and roared like thunder in unison with the screaming atmosphere.

"My elders, you are witnessing the birth of Tyranacus." A hiss of laughter escaped Trident's lips. "But wait. It has not yet fully formed."

"Fully formed, Master? What do you mean?" Aralynn asked.

"Watch!" Trident's eyes widened as he stared in awe at his creation.

Jimmy could smell rain approaching, but there was something different about it, like it was mixed with petrol or ammonia. When he glanced back at the beast, he was certain it had grown ever so slightly. Then, in front of his shocked eyes, Tyranacus doubled, tripled, quadrupled in size. The monster grew ten times its original size, the hard, dry, lifeless ground beneath his feet starting to crack and buckle under the immense weight.

As it flexed its muscles, the beast's sharp black toenails curled into the dusty ground, leaving deep furrows. With one last surge of growth, the ground gave way, forming an immense gorge. The creature sank into the hole, jammed up to its waist. Tyranacus roared in fury as it thrashed and flailed its arms, dragging its sharp nails along the floor, but the ground couldn't hold the beast's colossal weight. The creature's power began to leak into the walls of the newly formed gorge and they ignited in flames.

Tyranacus' eyes and nails sparked with purple flashes of electricity. When it clenched its fists, the dripping red sky became covered with thick, ominous black clouds. A fresh, clean breeze swirled past Jimmy's face as the first droplets of water bounced off the ground. When the second droplets hit, he heard the ground hiss, and a tiny plume of smoke filtered into the air. *Acid rain?* Jimmy thought. *Good thing we're inside the protective dome.*

The heavens opened, releasing a monsoon of acid-filled water that seemed to cover the entire planet, melting the man-made buildings and structures. Snarling, the beast clapped its hands together, igniting the rain droplets into a blaze of fire. Billows of thick, toxic smoke filled the air.

Tyranacus' eyes were charged with frenzy as storm after storm swept across the earth like a plague of locusts devouring everything in their path, only all this stemmed from one almighty beast. Jets of lightning flashed through the air, smashing into the ground. Volcanos erupted, flooding the lands with rivers of lava. Oceans ruptured, sending tsunamis to flood the shores, while hurricanes swirled, shredding the lands, destroying everything in their paths.

Then … in the blink of an eye, it was over.

As quickly as it had been created, the world was destroyed. A hollow, deathly silence filled the air, while a thick, congealed fog encased the whole planet like a shadowy gloved hand. From space, Earth would resemble a blazing rock, an inferno of fire, a raging tempest in the centre of the universe.

The firestorm of rain stopped, and the skies cleared. Jimmy heard Trident release a breath filled with great sadness.

The Council of Elders stared at the massive destruction, horror written in their expressions. Lord Trident himself appeared the most affected. Not a single word was uttered in what, to Jimmy, felt like an eternity.

Finally, Lord Trident spoke. "My elders, you have witnessed the raw power of my beast. It will save this wor—"

The elders were focused on Trident when he stopped mid-sentence. Jimmy, along with the elders, noticed a reflection in Trident's pupils growing larger as it stomped towards them. In unison, they snapped their attention back to the beast that had somehow managed to drag its way clear of the gorge. Its huge body sizzled in the harsh landscape, devastation it had caused. As it drew closer to them, the monster roared, sparks of electricity flashing from its fingertips. A long sliver of saliva splashed on top of the dome, soaking into the layers of the enchanted shell. Tiny fractures spread from that area, followed by the sound of cracking glass. With a deafening crunch, four thin lines of jagged splinters spread out, covering half the dome.

The sudden surge of fear and tension rising inside the dome became palpable. The group of elders had formed a line, their hands clenched into fists, ready for battle. All except for the long, thin frame of Lorratt Del-Vargo. Beads of sweat poured from his head, his shocked eyes wide, like a frightened rabbit staring into headlights.

"Master," Lorratt shouted, his hands shaking, "what is it doing? Stop it … use the pen. You must. You must be able to control it somehow!"

"What is wrong with you!" one of the other elders said. The tips of his flowing blond hair touched his collar, his muscles rippling beneath the white gown, his brown eyes filled with anger as he glared at Lorratt. "You have the power of the earth. Why do you fear this beast? Pull yourself together. Get ready!"

"Organtan," shouted Trident acidly. "Leave him alone. We have bigger things to worry about! I cannot control the beast. It is completely mindless. I didn't believe it would challenge the raw energy emanating from the dome, but I've made it too powerful. Now focus or this will be the end of us all, and this world!"

"No, Organtan is right!" shouted Lorratt, rubbing his face as he stared up at the beast. "I can do this … I will do this," he continued, clenching his fist. But Jimmy could hear the fear in his voice, see it in his eyes. He wasn't ready.

Tyranacus raised the black axe high above its head and smashed down with all its fury onto the weak spot. As the axe connected, the vibrations shook the structure, and the cracks in the dome widened.

Discarding its axe, Tyranacus' held one of its black fingernails to the sky, and the heavens opened, sending a surge of electricity into the beast. Turning back to the dome, the red creature released the powerful current into the weakening structure. The dome swayed and groaned under the enormous pressure but managed to hold firm.

Clapping his hands together, Tyranacus created two swirling tornados, one on either side of the hard shell.

As they crashed into the dome, Organtan shouted over the noise, "Get ready! Get ready!"

The dome, already damaged by spiderweb-like splinters, cracked wider, the outside air leaking into the pressurised shell. Tyranacus held its hands, still crackling with electricity, high above its head and smashed downward with all its might.

On impact, the dome exploded, raining shrapnel down on the elders, cutting and slashing their skin.

CHAPTER 13

The Children of Tyranacus….

Ignoring his pain, Organtan charged forward, unleashing shot after shot of power from his open palms. Jimmy could see the flexing muscles and strength behind every attack, which managed to stagger Tyranacus.

A lone javelin of lightning formed in Trident's right hand. He launched the weapon, and it sliced through the air, sinking into the top of Tyranacus' chest.

Roaring in pain, the beast grabbed the charged bolt and snapped it, but the electricity remained, surging through its blood.

Aralynn cut loose two spinning green fireballs, catching the beast in the chest. As it staggered backward again, the mighty frame of Roland Perrier fired an intense single beam of fire into Tyranacus' legs, causing the creature to lose its balance. When the monstrous beast fell, the ground beneath their feet shuddered.

A thick black cloud emitted from Huic's body, covering the monster as it lay on the floor. The cloud encased Tyranacus, causing the beast's skin to crack, then slowly wither and die. As it thrashed on the floor, none of the elders noticed the darkness creeping back into the sky.

As the beast's blood-red skin slowly and painfully turned black, it stared towards the sky, closing its eyes. Tyranacus used the last of its strength to create a blazing tornado, which hit the elders from behind, catching them unaware.

Trident, at the rear of the group, dived out of the way, grabbing a charcoal husk of what had once been a tree and hanging on with all his might. The harrowing winds pulled and dragged at his body, but he held on.

The tornado continued its destructive path towards a terrified Lorratt Del-Vargo, who'd frozen in place. The winds, controlled by the last of Tyranacus' strength, swept up the elder and threw him twenty feet through air, where he crashed hard into the ground below.

Seeing the tornado approaching him, Roland unleashed another stream of intense fire into the beast, weakening him further. The creature dug its claws into the earth, trying to keep its enormous body from sliding into the gorge.

With one final surge from Aralynn, it finally lost its grip. Tyranacus staggered backwards, falling into the waist-high gorge, where it was finally trapped.

With Tyranacus defeated, the tornado evaporated. Lord Trident dragged himself up from the floor and approached the gorge. As he watched, the creature's skin withered and crumbled away. "Huic, release your grip on it! We need it alive."

Huic ignored the request as thick black fingers of smoke drifted into the beast's mouth and down its oesophagus. Coughing and gurgling, Tyranacus' black eyes faded to white.

"I said to release him!" Trident shouted, clenching his fist and crushing Huic's hand with an invisible force.

The black cloud evaporated, and colour slowly returned to Tyranacus' frail body.

Huic stared angrily into Trident's eyes, clenching his fists as he shouted, "But we can't control it. It will destroy us all. Use the pen … destroy it!"

"Silence, Huic!" Trident shouted coldly. "You've done enough. I will not destroy the beast. I have a way to harness its power. Now go! Go and help Lorratt. You are no longer needed here."

Lorratt had collapsed some distance away, but Huic remained close enough to hear what Trident had to say. His expression turned ugly as he listened.

"My elders … my most precious elders and friends. We four have overcome a creature powerful enough to destroy this world. Now I must ask for your help once again. Help me to ensure the elders remain in total control of the beast so nothing like this ever happens again.

"Aralynn, with your fearless heart, Roland, with your pure might and power, and Organtan, with your recklessness and aggression, I propose we use some of our abilities to empower four humans who will be able to control this mighty beast. Every two thousand years, four children will be born and trained in the mystic powers of the universe. Tyranacus will be fully trained to do our bidding. The children will unleash the beast, and together they will destroy this world."

"But, Master," Aralynn said, wiping beads of sweat and black ash from her face, "what about Lorratt and Huic?"

Trident sighed as he studied the subdued beast, the destroyer of worlds. "Lorratt is weak and scared. The children need to be strong and fearless. When they receive a portion of your power, they will also be given your traits, your strength. But Huic … Huic is dangerous. There is evil lying deep within him, and I fear for his future. I will not allow one of the children to become that twisted and evil."

"Master, you said children would be born every two thousand years, but what will happen to the children born two millennia before them?" Organtan asked.

"An equally good question. They will each be given the power to control the mighty beast and destroy this world. But they will also need motivation. Each of them will be given a precious gift. Once the deed is done, and the clock of time re-starts, each of them will be offered a seat at the Council of Elders."

A loud groan came from the three elders, their expressions concerned.

"Fear not," Trident continued. "There will never be such a deal. Ultimately, the children will be cast into the world they helped destroy. They will walk the planet alone until the day they die." After a short hesitation, he said, "So, do we all agree?"

Expressions confused, the three members of the Council of Elders exchanged concerned glances, but none dared to openly challenge Trident's decision. Refusing to look him in the eye, they all nodded.

"Argh, good," Trident said, "a unanimous decision. Once the orbs are released, we will forge a prison for Tyranacus in the centre of the earth's crust, which can only be opened by the key." The end of the Rose Pen blossomed, and the tip ignited in a blaze of colour. "So marks the beginning of the new world, and the seed of the Children of Tyranacus!"

The heads of all four elders, including Trident's, snapped back, their eyes glazed over. Their bodies twitched as a faint mist was released from the pen and drifted into their nostrils. Their bodies went into spasm as four glowing spheres erupted from their skin. Their faces stretched as the orbs forced their way clear, then spun above their heads.

With a sharp inhalation, consciousness returned to the elders in time to see the four orbs float high above Sepura Castle. They moved gracefully above them, burning ten charcoal-covered zeros into the sky.

00/00/00 00:00

As a seed of life was cast over the world, the zeros gurgled, then clicked.

00/00/00 00:01

"My fellow elders. The seed of life has been spread across the world. The orbs will remain dormant ... dormant until the first Children of Tyranacus have been selected."

CHAPTER 14

A traitor in the midst: two days later….

Lying half-asleep, Majordomo heard a rapid patter of footsteps approaching his bedroom on an outside area of Sepura Castle. The echoes from those feet blended into his dream. In his dream, he walked through the luscious estate gardens, breathing in every delicious fragrance. His thoughts, his dreams, longed to be free. His only solace came from spending hours upon hours tending to the living plants of the garden.

As the footsteps drew nearer, a shadow swept past the door, jarring Majordomo from his dream. He wiped his eyes, then remained perfectly still, holding his breath as he listened.

The footsteps walked briskly away from his door, shoe heels clattering on the stone floor. As the fog cleared in his mind, his stomach lurched. *The Vantage Room. Whoever it is, they are headed for The Vantage Room.*

He jumped from his bed and quickly pulled on his trousers, then dropped his emerald gown over his head. The right side of the garment felt slightly heavy. Patting the pockets, Majordomo found the mound of purple sand he'd used earlier to ignite the fires. "I forgot to put the sand back," he whispered to himself, annoyed. He needed to keep the sacred sand safe, but he also needed to follow the footsteps of the intruder.

The sand could wait. *My master will never know,* he thought. *I'll find out what's going on and replace the sand before anyone ever notices.* Lingering in the shadows, he followed the footsteps.

As his eyes adjusted to the darkness, Majordomo crouched as he ran, peering around corners, but he found nobody there. He scratched his chiselled jaw, holding his breath as he listened. The mysterious footsteps continued a short distance ahead.

Scurrying silently through the corridors, he turned the final corner and caught sight of the flicker of a shadow through the doorway ahead. The footsteps echoed through the cavern as they climbed up the stone stairs.

Poking his head through the doorway, Majordomo saw a white-gowned figure climbing the steps ahead towards the Rose Door. The cavern was vast and dark, and he couldn't make out any features. He would need to get closer.

The air in the room carried the lingering sweet scent of roses. Looking ahead, Majordomo saw the intruder had already climbed the first thirty steps and was rapidly approaching the final thirty.

A cold breeze swelled up from the bottomless pit to his right, hitting Majordomo in the face. He held to the gold rail, his heart beginning to thump faster and his hands to shake as adrenaline hit his blood. Taking a deep breath, he suppressed his fear and climbed the steps in pursuit.

Once he reached the small platform, Majordomo glanced up, seeing the mysterious figure glaring down at him, emerald eyes glowing in the dark, raven hair flowing in the breeze.

"Huic!" Majordomo shouted in surprise. "What are you doing up here?"

Huic Ostiarius' face hardened, and the brightness in his eyes faded as the room became suddenly icy cold. "How dare you follow me! I am an elder. You are a mere servant … an experiment! A thing to populate this pitiful race."

The acid in his tone startled Majordomo, and he took a step back.

"Leave! Now!" Huic commanded.

Defiant, Majordomo remained focused. "I can't do that, Huic. Not until you tell me what you are doing. I'll need to make Lord Trident aware."

"Lord Trident." Huic laughed. "Lord Trident will not be able to stop me. Once I take the Rose Pen, I will rewrite this pathetic world he has created, and I will destroy Trident, taking my rightful place as the master of the council. Then we will see change!"

Majordomo's mind raced, taken aback by the revelation. "What do you mean? You can't." As realisation took root, Majordomo's voice became firm. "I won't let you!"

Huic released a sinister laugh that echoed through the cavern. "Try and stop me then!" He lifted his right hand and unleashed a charge of energy.

Majordomo dived out of the way, and it exploded on the base of the railing, snapping a section free from the concrete floor. The rest of the railing shuddered but held firm. The snapped metal flapped as it hung over the edge of the cavern.

Hearing the grinding of stone as the door to the Rose Pen room opened, Majordomo gathered his composure. He took a deep breath to help steady his nerves, then charged up the remaining steps to find Huic standing outside the open door. The pair collided, and Huic staggered back, crashing against the railing. The metal whined and creaked as small fragments of crumbling rock fell into the void.

Huic struck Majordomo in the face with his elbow, leaving a cut that streamed blood into his eye. Majordomo staggered backwards, dazed, as Huic released another charge of energy, catching him full in the chest. Slammed back hard into the railing, the thin metal legs snapped, then buckled under the immense strain, sending a section tumbling into the void, crashing into the walls as it fell.

Majordomo swayed, trying to catch his balance through the crushing pain in his chest.

Huic looked deep into Majordomo's eyes. He could see the silent plea for help, the raised right hand reaching out before his body surrendered to gravity and fell backwards over the edge. Dragged downward, Majordomo crashed into the side of the cavern, his green gown snaring on the jagged edge of the stuck railing. He gasped as the fabric ripped, dropping him a little further into the void. As his body twisted, a tiny grain of sand fell from his pocket into the pit below.

The dark void stirred and grumbled with rage, exploding into a blaze of purple fire. The intense flame washed over Majordomo's body, devouring his clothes, melting his skin. In agony, he screamed, "Huic! Huic, help me!"

Before he lost consciousness, Majordomo looked up and saw him … a smirking face, cold green eyes staring down.

The burning fabric of his robe tore again, jolting Majordomo. Before he could react, the whole pocket of purple sand dropped into the fire. The last thing he heard was Huic's footsteps running away before the cavern was filled with an almighty explosion, followed by endless screams of pain and terror.

CHAPTER 15

The grasp of power….

As the room outside detonated into a blaze of intense purple light, Huic dived into the blackness of the room holding the Rose Pen, his gown showered in flames. After he patted them out with his hands, he covered his ears to drown out the agonised screams, almost gagging on the smell of burnt flesh and magma wafting up through the air.

Then blessed silence.

Huic didn't allow regret to consume him. He was on a mission, and he knew from the start there would have to be sacrifices.

Scrambling backwards like a crab away from the burning cavern, he regained his composure and stood, dusting off his gown. As expected, the plant groaned and shook at the back of the room. Three vine tentacles slithered across the floor and up his legs, wrapping tightly around his waist. Having watched Lord Trident last time, he remained calm and perfectly still, although his body trembled with excitement. *Soon I will have the pen, and nothing ... no one will be able to stop me. How dare they not include me in the creation of Tyranacus and the children. How dare they! I am the most powerful of all, and now they will see. Now they will all see.*

The vines receded, and the room was cast into light. Huic climbed the white steps to the platform and carefully removed the glass case. He didn't have time to soak in the power. He knew the explosion would have woken the others. Time was of the essence. Taking the pen firmly in his grasp, he ran out into the smouldering cavern, down the steps and back along the winding corridors.

Once his feet sank into a luscious soft carpet just past Majordomo's room, he stopped and stood still, trying to control his wild emotions as he caught his breath. He glanced at the prize in his hands, knowing it had all been worth it. Smiling, he imagined sinking through the floor to the castle foyer.

As he drifted down, his foot slipped on the chequer-pattern of the marble floor in the foyer. Huic paused, checking all around the room, but he heard only silence. Walking confidently towards the wooden drawbridge, he could feel it, the raw power seeping through the pen into his hand, channelling along his arm.

"Huic!" a voice commanded from high on the platform above the wobbling staircase, echoing throughout the silence.

Huic's stomach tightened, but he kept walking, on a mission now.

"Huic, what have you done!" Lord Trident commanded again.

Huic stopped at the drawbridge and glanced behind him, seeing the other elders headed his way.

"What have I done!" he shouted coldly. "What I should have done a long time ago. I'm seizing power. I will re-create this world in my image! I will be the ruler of this pathetic race. You, Lord Trident, are weak! You gave these … these people everything, and how did they repay you? They destroyed your precious world, forced you to raze it to the ground. Then what? Do you punish them? No! Of course not. You simply re-start life again!

"You and your elders claim to be just, claim to be strong. But I can see it now. You are weak. My spirit should have been used to create Tyranacus … or at the very least one of the children. But you gave me nothing. Nothing at all. That will be your downfall."

Lorratt Del-Vargo and Aralynn filtered into the room behind Trident, glaring downward at Huic, their eyes pulsing with rage. "We have found him, Master," Aralynn said. "He is alive, but only just. He is badly burned. I fear he may not make the night."

Lord Trident breathed out a sigh, his eyes focused solemnly on the floor. Nodding, he spoke quietly, "Thank you, Aralynn. Please do what you can for him."

As the two elders left, Trident turned his attention back to Huic, his expression disheartened. "I am sorry, Huic. I've tried to be fair to you … to you all. You saw what happened to Nola. This new world was a chance to start again. But we can never go back after this."

Huic could see the slight sparkle of tears in Trident's eyes. His regret, the hurt.

"Huic, you do not need to run away. You have the pen, use it … use it here."

Anger swelled deep inside him. "Don't patronise me, Trident! I have the power in my hands. I'm the one holding the aces."

A faint smile of hurt spread across Tridents face, but his eyes narrowed as he said, "Then please use it."

"Argh," Huic screamed. "You no longer control me!" His arm swung around, holding the pen aloft in front of him. He looked up, seeing the sad expressions of his companions, his friends. With a deep breath, he swished the pen in the air as though he was the maestro conducting an orchestra.

He moved his hands like an artist painting a picture, but nothing … nothing happened. *Why?* he thought as his stomach twisted with fire. *Why isn't it working? I have the pen. It must be the room. He has done something!*

"What have you done! What is going on!" Huic demanded.

"I'm sorry, Huic. The pen will only work with my bloodline. Only me or one of my descendants can wield its power. I'm afraid your efforts here have sadly been wasted."

With a clap of Trident's hands, thick, black metal chains burst from the floor, clasping tightly around Huic's wrists and ankles. Huic felt sick, lightheaded, as the Rose Pen fell to the floor. The colour drained from his face as the metal chains drained his energy, and his skin withered and started to die. He collapsed to his knees, too weak to stand.

"They are *Drain of Life* chains. They will drain your powers and keep you weak until you have been sentenced."

*

Drained of energy and unable to lift his head, Huic struggled to keep his eyes open. His knees throbbed on the hard, slippery surface of the platform in the middle of the Council of Elders.

Tilting his head, he saw his vacant seat. The second one from the top.

"Huic Ostiarius, you are charged with the heinous crimes of theft, destruction, and worst of all, treason. How do you plead?"

Barely able to think, his mouth dry as sandpaper, his body riddled with pain, Huic just wanted this ordeal to be over with. "Guilty," he rasped.

"My fellow council members," Trident said with authority and power, "you witnessed the unfortunate events. Huic was in possession of the Rose Pen, and we have since seen the grave extent of Majordomo's injuries when he tried to stop him. How do you find the accused? Guilty or not guilty?"

There was a moment's pause before the voices raised one by one.

"Guilty!"

"Guilty!"

"Guilty!"

"Guilty!"

"Guilty!"

"Guilty!"

"Guilty!"

Rising from his seat, Lord Trident spoke with authority, but also with a hint of sadness, "Huic, you once described a punishment for the people of Earth. A punishment that in death, their souls should be locked in an Unearthly Prison for all eternity. Huic Ostiarius, your powers of an elder will be stripped. You will be cast into the Unearthly Prison as the Gatekeeper of life and death. You will collect the lost souls. Every two millennia, when the Children of Tyranacus are born, you will collect them and bring them to Elksidian Forest. I will grant you some power for this vital role, but nothing near the power to challenge me again! Now rise."

The chains dragged Huic to his feet and held him firmly in place.

"You will be cast into the Unearthly Prison through the sweltering void outside this room, the same void you allowed Majordomo to fall into."

Distressed, Huic groaned as he lifted his pleading gaze to the other council members.

"But, Lord Trident, the fires will burn him alive," shouted Rosaland Fellaini.

"Silence," Trident commanded. "May this be a lesson to you all."

As his youthful looks slowly filtered back into his body, the slackness in the chains tightened before they dragged Huic out of the room. Strengthened by the rejuvenation of his body, Huic pleaded, "Please, Lord Trident, I am sorry. You don't need to do this. I accept my punishment. I will do anything you ask. I'll go to the Unearthly Prison … but not like this. Please, please."

Trident responded coldly, "I understand Majordomo also pleaded. Did you listen?"

With a flick of Trident's wrist, the chains threw Huic over the edge into the void, the emptiness filled only with the crackling roar of flames below. In agony, Huic screamed as Lord Trident and his fellow elders sealed the gateway. As the last remnants of the flame diminished, the cavern was once again covered in a veil of darkness.

*

Jimmy was snapped back to reality as his mind leapt from the book and re-entered his body.

Taking a moment for the fog to lift from his mind, he stared down at the dry brown and yellow pages as the black video square in the middle gradually faded.

The pages of the book flicked back to the start. The start where the raven-haired young man once stood, the man shrouded in evil and menace. Now Jimmy understood. Grinning back from the page, the pure embodiment of evil, was the focus of Jimmy's vengeance. As his anger swelled, a green flame ignited around Jimmy's body.

There, looking back from the page, draped in his shredded cloak, was the skinless, bony body of the Gatekeeper.

CHAPTER 16

The visit that shaped the future….

Argon's booming, authoritative voice awoke Higuaín from her daydream. She checked around quickly to see if anyone had noticed her lack of attention. She recalled vividly that day four years ago when she'd run through the museum filled with joy and euphoria … before dragging open the Eclipse portal. There, fast asleep inside, had been a grey-haired, frail old man, clinging to the last strands of his life … a life spent wandering the devastated Earth alone. Higuaín remembered how her hand had trembled as she put the last drop of the *Elixir of Light* onto Argon's dry, cracked lips.

The effects weren't as instantaneous as she'd expected. Instead of the life surging back into his blood, the elixir took months. Slowly, day by day, Argon's blistered skin began to flake off, leaving only vibrant, bright pink flesh underneath.

Higuaín remembered the months of rehabilitation. Once the fibres in Argon's legs had knitted back together, he had to relearn how to walk. She'd heard him say over and over that he couldn't remember the last time he'd walked without a limp, or the need for that silly cane with the owl head on the top.

She remembered further back, to the pain visible in his eyes when he'd finally released the Light Dwellers from their eternal sleep. She had heard the roof of her own stone capsule grind open, and the thick fog that had encased her mind was lifted. Opening her eyes for the first time in centuries, she stepped onto the stone floor of the museum, her legs like rubber, just in time to see Argon collapse to the floor, the last of his life fading away.

But look at him now, she thought, taking in every detail of his face. The pain in his blue-grey eyes told her every inch of his struggles. She stared at his smooth skin, his fine chiselled jaw, and scruffy brown hair hanging just above his collar. Argon continued to speak as he ruffled the side of his hair. Higuaín thought about how thin and dry his short grey hair had been before she gave him the seed of the Palletine flower.

His muscles flexed beneath the tight black shirt every time he moved, but the most noticeable detail about him was his charisma … his leadership skills. He'd refused to accept defeat, coming up with detailed plans to make the army of Light Dwellers as strong as they could be, and the first thing he did was find them a new lair.

From her seat at the solid oak table, Higuaín looked around the small, yet homely cottage. In the living room area, twigs and logs crackled gently in a roaring fire. Hung above the mantel were the heads of all manner of animals hunted by the previous owners. The heads had scared her right from the start. It felt like they were watching her every move. No matter where she went in the room, their empty black eyes followed her, stared at her.

The smell in the cottage was a mixture of dried fur, old burned wood, and air from the moors seeping in through the gaps. The furniture, and even the floors, were all made of solid, dark brown oak created by a master carpenter, and made to last for the life of the cottage.

"So, Higuaín, have you been following Jimmy Threepwood?" Argon asked.

Higuaín heard the words, but they sounded distant, almost like an echo.

"Higuaín!" Argon said again.

She could feel the eyes of the others staring back at her. A gentle kick to her leg brought her back to the present, and she shook her head and looked up, sucking in a sharp breath. "Urm, sorry, I was deep in thought. What did you ask?" She offered a quick, grateful smile to Dravid for the nudge.

Stratos groaned as he slammed his boulder-like fists on the table. His chair squeaked as he dragged it forward.

"I asked if you have any update on Jimmy Threepwood?"

"Yes, Jimmy," Higuaín replied. "He asked for a few weeks' leave from his training to visit his mother back at Moutbatten Close. I've been watching him for days. He's not really gone anywhere, but something did happen, something a little strange. Two nights ago, a cloaked woman knocked on his door and handed him a book? It was pouring down rain, and the woman looked visibly terrified of something. She kept looking back over her shoulders into the darkness. She only stayed a few moments. I tried to follow in the shadows, but she disappeared, and I went back to watch Threepwood."

"Thank you, Higuaín," Argon said. "What did Jimmy Threepwood do with the book?"

"That bit was really odd. As I walked back to the house, the power in the street went out. Every house was black except Jimmy's room. Through the window I could see a flickering silver light, as if he were watching a movie."

Shifting her gaze to Shimmer, she could see he was trying to speak when—

Boom! Boom! Boom! came three hard knocks on the wooden door. The force of the strikes caused the door to rattle and the hinges to shake.

All eyes diverted sharply to the door, and Higuaín could see everyone holding their breath. Argon put his finger to his lips and directed everyone to move silently from the table. They crept into a dark corner of the room and crouched next to a wooden wall panel.

Dravid passed his palm over the wall. With a groan and hiss of hydraulic gas, the panel slid open, revealing a small, damp, hidden passage covered in layers of dust and sticky cobwebs. A stale odour drifted out of the narrow passage as one by one, flaming torches ignited on the wooden beams, the cobwebs crackling as the fire singed them.

Higuaín stared at the cottage door, poised to bolt into the hidden passage. She could feel the worry and anxiety from everyone as she whispered, "Who's that? Nobody knows we're here?"

Eyebrows raised, Dravid looked back, pursing his lips as he shrugged.

Boom! Boom! Boom!

"Stratos," Argon whispered sharply, "grab your axe and follow me … quietly!"

Argon crept towards the window, trying his best to avoid the creaking floorboards. He nearly jumped out of his skin at the next hard knocks.

Boom! Boom! Boom! Harder, faster this time.

Blowing air from his cheeks, Argon glanced over his shoulder to make sure Stratos was still behind him, then he gently pulled aside the edge of the curtains to look outside.

He could only make out the shadowed shapes of gnarled trees through the thick mist crawling across the moors. Arching his neck for a better view, Argon stared at the doorway, but saw nothing. There was no one there.

Boom! Boom! Boom! pounded the door again.

Argon looked again, pulling the curtain open a little wider, but there was still nobody there. Blowing out a breath, he walked to the door and lifted the metal latch. The hinges creaked as it opened. Still no one there. He opened the door further, and a furry black bat burst into the cottage, heading straight past Argon to flit around Stratos's head, slashing and clawing at his matted red hair.

Swiping at the bat with his axe, Stratos missed, and the axe slammed down hard on the wooden floorboards.

The bat crashed into the sideboard filled with plates and cups, sending them crashing across the floor. Higuaín dived out of the way, sending two of the kitchen chairs sprawling. As the bat circled Shimmer, then Dravid, the pair swatted at the creature, but it bit Shimmer's hand, then flew off, bouncing into the walls and sending a stuffed dear head tumbling to the floor.

The bat approached Argon, swinging around to hover in front of his face, and gave an ear-piercing shriek. Argon responded, not in aggression but by lifting and opening the palm of his hand. Hovering at neck height, the bat burst into flames. From the smouldering ashes, a white, perfectly folded white note dropped into his hand.

CHAPTER 17

The Eden Spire....

L ooking up at the carnage ahead, Higuaín walked towards Argon, crunching over the broken crockery which exploded under her feet, her gaze locked on the letter in Argon's hand.

"What is it?" shouted Dravid inquisitively, wrinkling his nose at the smell of burnt fur and ash. "How did it know you were here?"

"I don't know," Argon replied, "but I think its best we find out." The crisp, clean note rustled beneath his fingertips as he unfolded it, exposing long shaky letters in black ink.

Dear Argon,

I have enclosed some information which will assist you with your ... future plight.

I know of your quest to stop the four children, but ultimately you must destroy the beast Tyranacus to save this world.

Two thousand years ago, as one of the Children of Tyranacus, the elders bestowed knowledge upon you of how and why the beast was created. You know that three elders relinquished their powers to forge the mighty beast, and I am sure you are aware of their arrogance in thinking the beast would not turn on them.

To prevent this from happening again, four other elders, including Lord Trident himself, created a bloodline, a prophesy that every two thousand years four children would be born with the mark. They were destined to summon and control the beast as its power was unleashed.

But ... there were nine elders.

One of the remaining two, Huic Ostiarius, was punished for his actions and cast from the mortal world. The second, a weak, spineless man named Lorratt Del-Vargo, was seriously injured in the original battle to contain Tyranacus.

Lord Trident realised that if something should happen to any of the four children, the beast could not be controlled.

Once Lorratt had recovered, Lord Trident took a segment of his power and forged a sword. The sword, known as the Eden Spire, is the most fragile blade on the earth and could shatter with but the faintest touch. But the blade, if plunged into Tyranacus, would liquefy and poison his blood.

My gift to you, Argon, and your army of Light Dwellers, is the location of the secret enchanted weapon.

Use it wisely,

A black shadowy smudge mark signed the bottom of the page.

Argon turned the paper over, finding a pencil sketch on the back. He froze, his expression thoughtful.

"What does it mean, Argon?" Higuaín shouted.

"Argon!" Higuaín shouted firmly when she got no reply.

Forcing his eyes from the page, Argon slowly looked up, and a beaming smile spread from one side of his face to the other. He lifted the page and shook it. "This, Higuaín, this is what we have been waiting for. This is the chance to destroy Tyranacus once and for all!"

*

As Jimmy made his way towards Sepura Castle, the solid wooden slats of the drawbridge clattered and clanked under his boots. Walking alone, he turned his thoughts to his mother and how he'd left his house. His mother had handed him his cleaned and perfectly pressed robes, still warm from the iron. She'd overfilled the iron again, spilling water on the material, leaving it slightly damp in spots. He remembered her joyful smile, but Jimmy knew it had been a brave front. She tried to hide her real feelings, but he could see it in her eyes. Once Jimmy left, she would be all alone again, sad and lonely in this house made for a large family.

Jimmy remembered that awkward moment right before he left, not knowing if he should hug and kiss her goodbye. He felt angry at himself for just smiling and walking away. He swore next time he would try harder to break through the unease affecting their relationship. Growing up, it had been empty ... cold ... hollow in the house. But now, it was filled with warmth and the illusion of colour. Nobody had changed anything, or even painted, but it just seemed brighter, lighter, a hint of a loving glow.

Jimmy's eyes shifted to the right side of the drawbridge to the wooden handrail. He remembered when the shadowy phantom had pushed him against the rail and snapped it, sending part of it into the black sea. Professor Arual had used magic far beyond his capabilities to fish it back out and reconnect the severed metal. It was that night that he first met him, his mirror image. This translucent Jimmy had sat patiently on the bed as their thoughts merged.

'Jimmy... I am you! Well, a part of you at least. Think back to the day shortly after your father died, when you returned to Elksidian Forest. You were learning a conjuring spell, but you were not ready. Overwhelmed with sadness and anger, you kept aimlessly repeating the spell over and over'

'You were filled with so much rage, sadness, and a desire for revenge that you forced your goodness out of your body, leaving a twisted, power-mad version of yourself behind. I am that goodness, Jimmy, and I will never leave you. I just hope that one day your path will become clear and you and I can merge back together.'

Deep inside, Jimmy knew which path he had taken. He had known since the very moment he turned his back on Higuaín and selfishly refused to give even the smallest drop to save Argon … but he had to live with his decisions.

"Jimmy!" an excited, high-pitched voice echoed from deep within the castle entrance.

Breaking free of his troubled thoughts, the first thing Jimmy saw were her sparkling emerald eyes. He didn't know how to react, his arms hanging awkwardly by his sides.

Talula clattered along the bridge, flinging her arms around his neck, acting as though she had not seen him in years. He basked in the smell of her hair. It smelt of midnight rose, a sweet purple flower from the castle gardens. He noticed her new hairstyle and thought it suited her pear-shaped face. When they'd first met in the forest, she had worn her hair long and straight, flowing down the middle of her back. But now it was cut and feathered, curling over her shoulders.

"Jimmy, it's great to see you," Talula said, barely taking a breath. "Quick, come on, let me show you the castle. Look what they've done to it."

Talula dragged him into the entrance, nearly pulling his arm from his socket. The caustic scent of bleach and antiseptic slapped him in the face and soaked into his skin. The toxic fumes burned his throat and chest, making it difficult to breathe.

Crossing the threshold, Jimmy stepped onto the solid stone floor, forgetting all about the horrible smells as it scraped downward under the weight of his foot. Pressure on the slab ignited floating green flames high in the air, bringing every detail of the majestic room to life.

He stared upward at the vibrant painting on the ceiling, thinking about the Sistine Chapel in Rome. But the similarities ended as the grand painting started to move, alter, and twist.

Jimmy smiled as a black-robed boy slowly morphed into an antlered dear. A second boy transformed into an acid-green scorpion, slashing its poisoned-tipped tail into a creature Jimmy could only describe as the body and legs of a spider, and the upper body of a hideous blue man. The eight glowing red eyes spread across the creature's face winced in pain as the tail sliced through its shoulder, hurling green splatters of blood into the air.

The fine painting on the ceiling clouded over, replaced by the raw thrashing power of an ocean surf battering jagged rocks. The sound of the ocean swirled around the castle, poking and pulling at Jimmy's temporal lobe before subtlety altering into a beautiful, harmonic song that lulled Jimmy's senses.

Completely relaxed now by the delightful music, Jimmy watched as three beautiful angel-faced mermaids sprang from the water like elegant swans and sat on the rocks, beckoning to three boys wearing black robes to step into the deadly, thrashing sea. The boys' eyes were lost in a trance, ensnared by the radiance of the mermaids.

The images quickly altered, replaced by a horrendous wailing, high-pitched scream as the beautiful face of one of the mermaids melted away, becoming vile and twisted, blood dripping from her fangs.

Talula grabbed his arm, breaking him from his trance.

Panting, his hands and face clammy with sweat, Jimmy forced his gaze from the awful painting.

"You okay, Jimmy?" Talula asked softly.

Trying to calm his heart rate, he glanced upward again and saw the image change to the day he and his companions had climbed the wooden fence through the fuzzy perception filter and defeated the golden defender Aventis. The picture misted over, showing Jimmy knelt down, haunted by the ghosts of his power as he stared longingly at his hands.

"Jimmy!" Talula asked again.

"Urm, I'm okay," he said, running his fingers over his face. "I just saw a glimpse of something."

"What?" Talula asked.

"I'm not sure," he replied, glancing up again. "I don't know if it was all from the past or some of it from the future."

Taking a firm grip of Jimmy's hand, Talula asked, "Well, what do you think of the place?"

CHAPTER 18

The scar....

Arhythmic hum vibrated across the polished black and white tiled floor as hundreds of tiny transparent hands grew from below the surface. Working in magical unison, the hands, each firmly clutching a yellow cloth, scrubbed at the castle floor, collecting every tiny particle of dust and grime.

The floor squeaked and squealed with every single wipe as a fine cleaning mist was released into the air to rain down on the surfaces, giving it that final high gloss. At the far end of the room, hands climbed and snaked around the two rows of columns reaching from floor to ceiling, scrubbing and polishing as they climbed. Jimmy had only ever seen the room covered with old dusty sheets, but now the room sparkled in the light beaming through the clean windows.

"Isn't it amazing," Talula said, seemingly captivated by the flowing, cleaning hands. "It started right after you left. Professor Arual thought the castle needed a good cleaning, and the hands have been working nonstop ever since."

The smell of bleach and polish continued to burn Jimmy's eyes, making him feel dizzy as he walked into the middle of the room. With a click below his feet, six green projections burst into life in a circle around him, showing monumental moments in history. As he watched, he caught the sudden flicker of movement in the shadows near the door, and the slither of movement across the floor.

Talula grabbed his hand as he stared into the darkness. "What is it?" she asked.

"I don't know." He frowned. "I thought I saw someone."

"Come on," Talula said impatiently. "We've been waiting for you. Majordomo asked to see you as soon as you arrived. There's something going on in the castle, but no one will tell us what. Professor Potts and Majordomo were insistent that our training continue straight away, and we need to be ready."

"Need to be ready?" Jimmy asked.

"Whatever has happened, they looked spooked. A few days ago, they considered sending someone to come and fetch you early."

"And you have no idea what?" Jimmy asked, thinking back to the visit from Madam Shrill, the fear in her eyes, the quaver in her voice, and the blood on his hands the day he found her.

"Not really," Talula replied, "but I have been listening to Professor Potts, and I believe it's got something to do with the disappearance of Professor Tinker and Madam Shrill. They keep repeating the name Imjimn-Ra, but there's something else. They keep mentioning another. Sometimes they call him the Blackness, or the Shadow. They're petrified. You can see it in their eyes when they mention him. I've never seen them scared of anything. They don't say much, but whoever that is, it's clearly affecting them. Even the elders look scared."

"The Shadow?" Jimmy asked,

"Yeah, they keep saying that the darkness is approaching."

"Have you asked them about it?"

Talula paused. "Percy asked Professor Potts last week, but he snapped at him, acting furious. He yanked his office door clean from the wall and told him to get out. Come on, Jimmy, we'd better go find them. We need to see when they want us in class next."

Jimmy followed Talula as they passed through the flickering projections. He was thinking about Madam Shrill running through the darkness, and what she had told him.

'He wouldn't tell me all the details, but he did mention a plot to destroy the elders by someone close to us ... a friend.'

Jimmy felt a cold chill crawl down his spine, and the hairs on the back of his arms stood on end. He looked back just in time to see the darkness in the corner morph into a human figure. Harry Hopkins stepped into the light, his spiky brown hair now shaved. The newest addition to his face was a scar running vertically from his eyebrow down to his cheek.

Surprised, Jimmy quickened his pace and tugged at Talula's sleeve. He glanced back to see Harry lurking in the shadows, watching them. "Talula, what's the matter with Harry?"

Talula shrugged. "He's been acting strange ever since the flaming bat brought him a letter. It had a black wax seal, and when he opened it, he went white as a ghost. He's been acting odd ever since.

Jimmy sighed. "Only two weeks away and the place falls apart."

Jimmy had just reached out to grab the firm railing either side of the Emerald Staircase when Professor Will Potts suddenly appeared from deep within the wobbling steps, startling Jimmy and Talula. They both bowed down immediately, dropping onto one knee.

Jimmy lifted his eyes and glanced discretely at his former school friend. It had been four years since Will had stepped over the threshold into the castle, a glowing ruby crystal dangling from his neck. Back then, he'd had youthful, good looks and a twinkle in his eye. But that felt like such a long time ago.

This looked like a husk of the Will Potts Jimmy had known. His shoulder, elbow and knee bones poked through the worn robes. Sickly grey skin hung from his gaunt face; his eyes were bloodshot from lack of sleep. His once perfectly combed, parted hair carried streaks of silver running like mole tunnels through it. An empty vessel used by Lord Trident to do his bidding.

Pursing his lips, Jimmy gave a slight shake of his head, thinking, *Don't worry, my friend. I'll find a way to get you out of this mess ... even if it's the last thing I ever do.*

"You are late, Threepwood!" Professor Will Potts boomed. "We've been waiting patiently for you. I gave you a leave of absence, but now you are pushing it! Don't let it happen again! Do you understand?"

The ruby-red stone hanging loosely around Professor Potts neck clouded as Lord Trident's familiar face pushed through the murk, demonstrating that it was him in total control of Professor Potts' body. With a snap of Professor Potts' fingers, both Jimmy's and Talula's bodies became rigid and unresponsive to their will.

As their eyes glazed over, the last memory Jimmy had was seeing Percy and Harry being dragged towards them before they were all sucked through the Lorda Door.

CHAPTER 19

Finally, we meet the professor....

Jimmy felt lost in a deep, dark tunnel as distant, murky voices became louder, crisper, clearer.

"Jimmy," the voice whispered, and he felt his shoulder being yanked and pulled repeatedly. His body felt heavy, unresponsive, as though it belonged to someone else. He tried to force his eyes open, but his eyelids felt weighed down with tiny stones.

His head rocked side to side, and he finally got his eyes slit open enough to let in a little light. With a sharp inhalation, he scrambled shakily to his feet and crashed into a bookshelf directly behind him. As books clattered to the hard-tiled floor, he took in his surroundings, growing slowly more alert.

His head pounded as Talula continued to speak. When his blurred vision finally cleared, he saw Harry helping Percy to his feet.

"Argh, you have arrived," a soft, happy voice said, coming from a storage cupboard at the far end of the room.

With an open book resting on the palm of his flat hand, an eloquently dressed man glided out, his feet barely touching the floor, or so it looked. Never taking his eyes from the book, he ran his spare hand through his curly silver locks as he said, "Don't worry, the groggy feeling will soon pass. You'll be a little disorientated and sick for a short while, then you'll be right as rain. It's because you have entered a new, more advanced part of you training, and your body is not yet used to the journey into this room."

The man looked up. "Oh, where's my manners. I am Professor Lorda. I'm going to be your teacher for advanced conjuration and creatures long since forgotten. Now please have a seat. There is much to learn."

Taking the seat next to Harry, Jimmy smiled as the professor bounced, almost waltzed, around the room without a care in the world. *What a breath of fresh air,* he thought. Since he had been in the castle, his teachers had been two twin green lizards, a giant Ogre, and of course the empty body of his former friend. But Professor Lorda was so different. Looking around, he found the room alight with vibrant colours, and the professor seemed kind and softly spoken.

Closing the book, Professor Lorda placed it on a thick wooden desk in front of the storage cupboard, then he rummaged around in the pockets of his chalk-covered golden gown which swept across the floor just above his ankles. Solid gold bars of a slightly darker material ran down the centre of the gown decorated with swirls of gold silk.

"Here they are," he said, opening his fist. "You are finally ready for your identity rings. These rings will merge with your life force and will not only provide access to deeper, more powerful spells, but they can also be used as homing beacons in case any of you should ever get lost.

"Percy, Talula and Harry," the professor shouted as he tossed three golden rings high into the air. "Hmm," he groaned, rummaging back in his pockets before searching around on the floor. "Strange. Threepwood, your ring seems to be … missing." He scratched his thick silver hair and muttered something under his breath whilst staring at the door.

The levitating ring spun and twisted, landing on its edge in Percy's palm. He ran his fingers over the rough, uneven metal. It felt alive, like a dragon snarling silently in the back of his mind. The words *Percy Timmins* were engraved all the way around. The ring felt as hot as molten lava yet didn't burn. The intense heat radiated through his body, invigorating his skin, and replenishing his energy stores. Percy glowed with power.

Percy slid the ring gently over the index finger on his left hand, where it sat snugly next to the *Ring of Vision,* which he had received from Iveco four years earlier for passing the deception trials. Running his finger over the two rings, he thought back to the countless number of times he had needed to use the *Ring of Vision* … to see even the slightest glimpse of the future. But nothing. It didn't even give a hint of foresight.

"Jimmy," Professor Lorda said, his expression puzzled as he scratched his right cheek like a cat with fleas. "Don't worry. I will use a spell to search the classroom and castle grounds for your ring. We'll find it very soon. However, it is very alarming that it is not here."

Lorda suddenly turned away from the group and mumbled under his breath, "No, go away! Not now! I will not release you." He coughed, trying to disguise his voice.

As they watched, a large lump grew under the professor's skin and slowly crawl around to his face, Talula elbowed Percy to grab his attention.

Panicking, Professor Lorda shouted again, covering his disfigurement as beads of sweat formed on his forehead. "No! Not now!" he shouted as he doubled over, grabbing his stomach in obvious agony. His stomach started groaning and grumbling.

"Professor!" Talula shouted, concerned, rising from her seat and pushing the attached wooden rest aside.

"No!" Lorda shouted, thrusting his arm forward to halt her movement. "Please stay back." His hands visibly shook, and the beads of perspiration were now trickling down his face. The professor suddenly collapsed to his knees, his body going into spasms. "No … not now."

Lorda glanced up at his wooden desk stacked high with piles of paper. He crawled on his hands and knees, then grabbed the wooden table and dragged himself up. "I can't resist … its hold is too strong." With a final thrust, Lorda sent papers, notes and maps flying through the air. He grabbed an old wooden mask with jagged edges, and three diagonal strips painted across it, and held it aloft.

Shocked by the events unfolding before their eyes, the students couldn't move. Their new teacher, so full of life and bounce, suddenly turned into a quivering wreck, scrabbling for a mask on the desk as though his life depended on it.

Clutching the mask in his hand, Lorda staggered across the room, crashing into tables and then the chalk board as he screamed, forcing the mask to his face.

Instantly, a cold wind sliced through the room. The mask came alive, crawling over his face and piercing his skin, injecting a dark inky substance. The watery liquid washed through Lorda's silver curls, turning it black and straight. Sharp fingernails grew long, and his bright yellow gown faded to black.

Raising his head, Lorda's eyes had also turned raven-black behind the mask, and a crooked smile was painted across the front.

The four students moved slowly towards the back of the room, sensing the evil leaking through Lorda's pores.

"That's better," Lorda croaked, his voice deep and raspy, slightly muffled by the mask. "It's nice to feel the raw power of the mask channelling through my veins now and again. And now your lesson truly begins," he shouted through the room. "Draagaaarr!"

The tiles next to his feet rumbled, then cracked and split as a giant, thick, slime-covered worm burst through the floor. Its circular mouth was covered in jagged, razor-sharp teeth as it slashed forward with its huge body at the children.

"Meet the Magworm," Lorda shouted, laughing at his demonic creation.

Harry dived out of the way of the thrashing head and gestured his hands on each side of his body to ignite his hands, but nothing happened. Astonished, he ducked the next attack as Talula ignited her hands. Her palms sparked and stuttered, but then faded to nothing as the Magworm smashed past chairs, sending them sprawling across the room, to slash at the corner of her shoulder.

"Did I forget to mention," Lorda roared, pointing with his long-nailed fingers, "those rings take time to charge and attune to your bodies. They suck away your powers until you can fully merge your life forces with them."

"But my ring is missing!" Jimmy shouted defiantly as his hands sizzled into life. He held a long crackling javelin in his clenched fist.

The Magworm coiled at the new threat, then in one motion, similar to a slinky toy tumbling down the stairs, dived forward with its mouth fully open, swallowing Jimmy whole.

CHAPTER 20

New powers are revealed….

"Jimmy!" Percy shouted, picking up a jagged chair leg that had snapped clean off during the struggle. He jabbed forward, prodding the cold-blooded creature's thick, slimy skin.

With its teeth still clamped to the floor, the creature groaned and churned. It gurgled, releasing its grip as it shot straight up on its spineless body. Black hairs over its body bristled as it glared down at the defenceless children.

Percy, Talula and Harry had picked up broken pieces of tables or chair legs and were thrusting forward, trying to hold off the creature.

The Magworm slammed its body into the ground and lunged forward in one swift movement, smashing through the classroom wall. Bricks crashed to the floor, casting a plume of dust into the air. Like a viper, it recoiled its body for a second strike, then once again dived forward, barely missing Talula.

Pulling free of the dust and rubble, the Magworm stood upright again, poised to attack, when an odd grumbling started again deep within its belly. With an almighty burp, foul green gas puffed out of its mouth, and it retched and spluttered. With a familiar hiss, the Magworm's belly sliced open from the inside, showering the children in thick, putrid ooze before it toppled to the floor in two pieces.

In the bottom half of the worm, his feet squelching in the slime, stood Jimmy, covered head to toe in gunk. The glow of his sword faded as it deactivated, leaving behind the foul stench of burnt flesh in the room.

Jimmy wiped his face and flicked the goo onto the floor with a splat, then turned when he heard Lorda laughing from behind his mask.

"You fools," Lorda roared. "That creature is a Magworm!"

Jimmy caught movement out of the corner of his eye and turned to see the top half of the decapitated creature begin to wriggle and move.

"If you cut it in half, both parts of the body will regenerate. Every time you slice off a piece, more will grow! It is the perfect weapon ... deadly and indestructible."

Jimmy lost his balance as the second half of the worm below his feet began to squirm and wriggle.

Suddenly the room was filled with screams and whines coming from Professor Lorda. His long black nails dug deep behind the mask as he shouted, "Noooo! I have had enough ... release ... your ... hold!" His skin stretched out as he tore the mask from his face and threw it to the floor.

Exhausted, Lorda dropped to his knees as the vibrant colours gradually returned to his skin and clothes. He shouted one last time, his hand splayed out in front of him, "Taardack Raal."

Jimmy ducked as a burning-red Pterodactyl sliced through the fabric of time and space, where it soared past his head, cutting clean through a newly formed Magworm poised to strike. Circling in the room, its razor-sharp wings cut into the wall, and the Pterodactyl screamed as it dived, hooking the two worms in its talons before it disappeared through another slice made into an unknown dimension.

Without a moment's hesitation, Jimmy followed the others as they ran to Lorda, pushing aside damaged tables and clambering over rubble.

With long, slow, deep breaths, Lorda struggled to open his eyes. "I … I'm sorry you had to see my other side, children. Sometimes I just lose control. At least now you have seen first-hand the new creatures you will be able to control. They are indestructible to any mortal weapon, and only the most powerful warrior can defeat them."

"But what happened? Where did they go?" Percy asked, filled with enthusiasm at the immense power within reach of his greasy fingers."

"The void," Lorda whispered. "The creature that took them is called a Grinderlar. They are the keepers of the void … the second dimension of empty space clinging to this realm."

Exhaling loudly, Lorda's eyes closed, the professor overcome by exhaustion.

*

Later that night…

Tossing and turning in his bed, Harry's feet kicked and thrashed through the air. Lorda's black wooden mask swirled and circled in his mind, prominent in a sea of empty blackness. As the mask swayed and dangled in front of his face like a puppet on invisible strings, Harry lashed out with his hands, scooping up only thin air.

Harry could see every grain, every layer of the ancient, rounded wood, even the three dirty streaks, an inch in diameter, running diagonally through the mask. The mask, or the wood, had dried out over the centuries and started to curl and split at the ends.

The empty hollow eye holes zoomed in closer and closer as they formed the faint outline of soulless yellow eyes. They glowed brighter and brighter as the mask faded into the emptiness. Sharp realisation washed over Harry's sleeping mind as he recognised their owners.

"No," Harry mumbled, thrashing his arms. "I had no choice. I was taken … the Gatekeeper collected me. I couldn't do anything about it."

Silence ensued for what felt like an eternity before a cutting voice sliced through the air, "You had a choice."

The wooden window frames burst open, slamming hard against either side of the wall, allowing a gust of cool night air to blast into the room. The sudden noise jolted Harry from his deep sleep. Before he got his bearings, he tumbled from his bed, crashing onto the hard floor. Panic set in when he couldn't untangle his body from the quilt.

Clawing the cover free, he stared frantically around the room, like an animal being hunted, ready to spring. As his eyes slowly adjusted to the darkness, and awareness returned, his breathing and heart rate slowed.

Hands trembling, he took in the open window and wiped his palm over his face, his clammy skin quickly cooling. With his stomach still churning, he focused on the light, reaching out with his left hand to fumble for the switch. The light flooded the room, chasing away the shadows, and his fears began to melt away.

Harry looked into all four corners of the room, rubbing the back of his neck, feeling silly for being scared of nothing.

But it seemed so real. I could feel his breath on my face. Why now? What did the High Delf want with me after all this time? I meant what I said. I didn't have a choice. The Gatekeeper took me.

The words from the dream created a ball of anxiety which slowly crawled down the back of his throat. *'You had a choice.'*

Gathering his composure, his mind clicked into gear. *The library,* he thought. *The book of my life. I need to find out what happened to them. I need to find out what happened to the Delf.*

CHAPTER 21

The Delf....

Closing his bedroom door quietly, Harry glanced at his room number. A large black metal number 2 shaped like a viper.

He closed his eyes and thought of the library. With a gurgle and a slurp, the ground below his feet turned to mush and he seeped into the carpet.

The hinges squealed and groaned as he used his shoulder to force open the heavy wooden door to the library. He groaned at the stale, chalky taste that flooded his mouth. Coughing to clear his lungs, he stepped into the cold, dank room and scurried to the centre. Nothing happened. He still had vivid, and painful, memories of the first time he'd entered the library. The mound of books had come crashing down on his head. He had learned from that mistake and it wouldn't happen again.

He stared around the deserted room. It had been months since he had seen Madam Shrill, and the library was lost without her. *I wonder where she is?* He thought back to the weeks and weeks of endless searching the elders had made them do. Traipsing through all types of weather through the surrounding fields, grass, and shrubbery, but she was never found. He thought back to Jimmy and that knowing look in his eyes. But if Jimmy knew something, he never said.

Walking to the wooden counter, he lifted the hinged shelf that locked it vertically in place. Harry stood on his tip toes as he reached up with his fingers to wipe the dust away from the bindings of the neatly placed books. His vision blurred when dust fell into one of his eyes, stinging. He tried to wipe it clean, but the discomfort remained, and he was forced to continue looking using only one eye.

The Life of Eunice Aurabella

There was a clear gap, a missing book, before *The Life of Eunice Aurabella* but Harry skipped his finger over the gap and wiped the rest of the books one by one in order:

The Life of Roland Perrier
The Life of Organtan Carnevale
The Life of Oler Roindex
The Life of Talula Airheart
The Life of Percy Timmins

Pausing for a moment, hovering over Talula's book. he grabbed it, then stopped himself, grabbed it again, but finally decided to leave it. He needed to find out about the Delf.

Running his finger past Percy Timmins, he finally reached his book. Pulling it from the shelf, he slammed the heavy book on the table. A tiny black spider scuttled away as he wiped away a thin sheet of dust. Clicking on the desk lamp, he held his breath in expectation and opened the book to the first page.

The page was filled with a mixture of black and white and modern pictures full of vibrant colours. Underneath each picture were two faded pencil lines, and written above them using a quill, the date of the photo and the person captured.

Underneath the first picture of a woman running through a forest was the name *Helena Hopkins,* and the date *17th September,* but the year had faded away.

The images remained frozen on the page, though somehow still came alive in Harry's mind, his senses picking up the fragrances first, then the textures. They pulled at his spirit, allowing him to feel what the people felt, and to see through their eyes. As the story unfolded, moving from picture to picture, his mind hopped from body to body.

The lone woman's feet squelched in a thick slushy puddle of mud, splashing the hem of her ankle-length gown as she scurried through the wood. The sleeve of her gown snagged on the thorny brambles, creating runs in the fabric. The ground rumbled beneath her feet as the sound of galloping horses drew nearer. The air filled with the victorious cheers of at least six rowdy men.

Panting heavily, the female pressed on, ducking branches and overhanging shrubs. The jagged thorns and protruding twigs slashed at her calves, a faint trickle of blood running down her legs, but she continued … she continued at whatever the cost.

Running deeper into the forest, her path covered by dense woodland, she didn't see the fallen log. Catching her ankle, she tumbled and staggered forward, doing all she could to keep her balance. In the blink of an eye, she fell, twisting her body to protect the precious bundle tucked snugly under her right arm. Crashing hard to the soaking floor, she skidded on her left shoulder, slicing through the thin fabric and grazing her skin.

Panic filled her heart as she pulled herself shakily to her feet. She unravelled the package, staring down into a tiny, bright-eyed baby boy who was oblivious to the world around him.

"It's okay, my love … not much longer," she whispered, wincing as the droplets of rain that fell from the end of her nose hit her grazed shoulder, stinging.

The horses whinnied as they approached. Terror ignited a fire in her stomach, and she limped on with the last of her strength. Bursting through an opening, she fell to her knees next to a muddy track worn into the forest over time.

She twisted, trying to protect her precious bundle from the splash of cold water as six horses thundered past. The black horses galloped on into the night, all except for the rider at the rear. Pulling back on the reins, the horse's hooves skidded to a stop, and it blew condensation from its nose. In the dead of night, the heavy breath looked like smoke billowing from a burning fire in the beast's soul.

As the horse clopped through the muddy water towards the lone female, she kept her head focused firmly on the floor, imagining its fiery eyes glowing an intense demonic red.

"You should be very careful who you try to stop in the dark woods! You never know who you will meet," the lone rider boomed.

"My Lord," the woman said softly, never once altering her gaze from the crushed shrubbery at her feet, rainwater pouring down her face. "I have come here in search of the lost Tribe of Assassins. The infamous Delf."

"The Delf?" the rider repeated inquisitively. "And what would you know of … the Delf?" He climbed down from the horse and stood before her.

"My Lord," the female said respectfully, but her voice and bottom lip still quivered with fear. She had no idea how the Delf would react to being stopped and identified. She knew there was a very strong chance they would silence her forever on the side of the road, but it was a chance she had to take.

"My Lord, I know that you are like ghosts, the unseen legend of this land. A guild whose name strikes fear with but a mention. I also know of one's perilous journey to the top of Mount Metus to invoke a contract for you to assassinate a target. The need for one to read from the script of the dead and to leave a sizeable sum of money. I also know that you, my Lord, are the High Delf, leader of the assassins, and the one who I have sought."

Her heart skipped a beat when she heard a knife being drawn slowly from a leather sheath. Breathing rapidly through her nose, she closed her eyes. *I've said too much. He can't leave me alive now. Why did I tell him so much?* Glancing up, she saw the hulk of a man was draped in a tight leather suit. A cowl covered his head with a mask spread across his mouth. His eyes were yellow, almost pulsing in the shadows.

"Knowing the sacred way to invoke our service, you decide to stop us here … on this highway. How did you know of our exact location? How did you know we would be passing here at this very moment?"

She froze, terrified, her gaze back on the floor. "Because, my master, I have a package for you." She pulled back the shawl, revealing the baby fast asleep in her arms. "I have been shown the boy's future, seen his destiny. I have seen what he will do, what he will become. I have been shown a glimpse of the future by a creature, by the Gatekeeper."

The instant the words left her mouth, the woman was sure she heard the rider gasp. He definitely took a step back, followed by the familiar sound of the knife being dropped back in its sheath.

"The Gatekeeper told me I couldn't control the boy's powers, and the only ones who could were the Delf. I made a pact with him to hand my only son to you to save the world. Please!" she begged, "you must take him. Please, it's the only hope for the world."

The woman heard the squeak of leather as the High Delf grabbed the reins of his horse and climbed back into the saddle.

"There's one more thing," said the woman. The cold caused pins and needles to set in in her legs, and she could barely feel her toes. "The Gatekeeper was concerned you may not be interested, but he told me to tell you of my son's gift."

"Gift?" the cowled assassin murmured.

"Yes, a gift that will have great benefits to your organisation. My son was born with the cloak of stealth. With but a mere thought, his body can fade into nothing, become a spirit … an apparition, an undetectable stealth assassin. An assassin under your control. Please, my Lord, please take him. Please help him. Help us all."

After a lengthy silence, the High Delf threw out a gloved hand. "What is the boy's name?"

A mixture of emotions erupted inside the woman, joy mixed with relief that her son's future could be prevented, but also great sadness that she may never see her son again.

"Harry, my Lord … Harry Hopkins."

CHAPTER 22

The Life of Harry Hopkins....

Harry's eyes moved over the pages from picture to picture. His mind could feel and see the data, but his body was rigid, locked in place. He felt like a wooden puppet with an arm up his back, moving his eyes for him.

His mind bounced from image to image, seeing the world for a second time through his own eyes, the images of his life with the Delf. From the moment he could walk, a sword had been thrust in his hand. He learned to master the weapon, to both attack and defend himself. He perfected the art of knife throwing, melee combat, and unarmed strikes. But the one he excelled in far above anyone in the history of the Tribe of Assassins was stealth. With the gentle manipulation of his mind, he could fade into the shadows, unseen by the naked eye, and this power was exploited and trained further with other similar skills such as lock-picking.

He watched as he grew older and more confident, teetering on the edge of arrogance. He watched on as his powers twisted his mind, making him headstrong. During training, he was like a coiled spring ready to explode. He had no control of his senses or surroundings and would constantly dive headfirst into dangerous situations. He was endlessly told and reminded of his actions, but his mind was clouded. Regardless of what the High Delf or his trainers told him, he always thought he knew better.

As the young Harry Hopkins grew older, the images moved to his first assassination, the fulfilment of his first contract. On his eleventh birthday, he was granted the rank of Delf.

"My fellow Delf," the High Delf boomed from his platform high above his army of assassins, speaking from the notes resting on his wooden podium. Harry Hopkins sat proudly to his left. The hall was lit only by the gentle flicker of ten candles, and a dirty black fog had crept in from the vents and settled on the floor like a carpet. At the rear of the hall, either side of wooden doors, sat two tall wooden racks overflowing with axes, swords, knives, and all manner of weapons.

"Are we alone?" the High Delf shouted ritually, the question used to start every meeting. With a nod of his head, two guards stood at the rear of the hall, either side of the wooden racks, and tapped the mental ends of their ceremonial staffs hard into the concrete ground twice.

Two similar knocks pounded on the outside of the wooden door to symbolise they were alone, for all members knew any less meant they were in danger. It was the outer guard's duty to warn of any danger and prevent entrance into the sanctuary.

"We are alone!" the two guards shouted in unison.

Speaking slowly, pausing before every word to create suspense before such a monumental moment, the High Delf said, "You are witnessing a rare event, something never heard of in the history of the Delf. A boy, Harry Hopkins, will be granted the honour of becoming a Delf at the age of only eleven. His skill at cunning and stealth are unmatched, and though headstrong, this will be nurtured and developed.

"For now, brethren, I wish you to stand as the newest brother of the Tribe of Assassins enters the tomb of Pactum, the sacred sanctuary, to receive his first orders from the Beholder ... the giver of contracts."

Harry rose nervously, surrounded by the rapture of applause. He looked down from the platform at the applauding assassins clad in their tight leather suits, gloved hands, faces covered in masks. Feeling uneasy, uncomfortable at this unusual attention, he looked at the lifeless stone wall to his left, at the hidden soulless hall far below the unsuspecting town of Chapforth. Ceremonial skulls hung from the walls. Shredded fabric dangled from the ceiling and flapped in the thin air.

A heavy hand crashed onto his shoulder. "My boy," the High Delf said. "The Beholder has personally asked for your installation to the Delf at this early stage in your life. He has a very special contract from important clients that only you, with your ... special skills, could achieve. As such, you have been appointed the rank of Delf, and I am certain this will set you on a path that will one day see you replacing me as the High Delf, leader of the Tribe of Assassins. But for now, my new brother, you must enter the tomb of Pactum. You alone must see who requires our services. Go, do not keep the Beholder waiting." He gave Harry a persuasive nudge forward.

As Harry approached, the stone wall grinded and scraped open, and he stepped into an empty, dimly lit room with four grey walls. Ducking instinctively as the door rumbled shut, an eerie, high-pitched voice echoed throughout the room, sending an icy chill down his back. The voice was loud, but at the same time distant, as though it echoed from another world.

"Harry Hopkinnnss," the voice whispered. "At my request, you have been enrolled early to the rank of Delf.

Never before has someone so young been given such responsibility. But neither did they have your special gift."

A giant face twisted and pushed its head from inside the wall in front of him. The bodiless face moved and groaned as it continued, "The Union of Monks has provided me with a contract. Their leader and head father has made decisions the other members do not agree with. They have provided a considerable amount of money to fulfil the contract. But don't be fooled. They have mystical powers far beyond your comprehension, and to attack one of the Union of Monks head on would be very foolish, and indeed fatal.

"This is why I need your ... particular skills. The head father is on a sabbatical in a cottage at a secluded location known only to the other monks. They have provided a map and the master key to the door. You must enter the cottage covered in stealth today in daylight and remain there locked in the wardrobe and watch his every movement. When you are sure he is asleep and at his most vulnerable, you will kill him. But ... this must be made to look like an accident. The details I shall leave to you. Once you have succeeded in your contract, you must return to me and you will be provided with your reward. Now go. Let the luck of the Delf be bestowed upon you."

Back in the library, Harry watched on as he moved to the next images in the book. He already knew the outcome, but he refused to look away. He watched on as every event unfolded in front of his eyes, forced to relive the moments in time.

Cloaked in stealth, Harry crept silently to the wooden cottage hidden miles from its nearest neighbour. He walked along the worn forest path, his hands shimmering in the sunlight, invisible to the naked eye. Like a chameleon, his skin altered to his surroundings. As he walked past a row of trees, his skin matched the colour and grain of the bark right down to the finest detail, even mirroring tiny gouges left by woodpeckers.

When he came closer to his target, he stopped to watch as a monk opened the front door, collected a chopping axe, and placed several blocks for kindling on an old tree stump. Holding his breath for fear of being seen, Harry waited, checking in all directions for potential escape routes.

Startled by the axe slicing through the wood, five birds scurried through the trees high above Harry, crashing through branches, squawking hysterically. Harry froze, his heart beating like a drum when the elderly monk looked straight at him, but his gaze continued to follow the line of the birds.

Re-adjusting the cable hanging from his waist, the monk rolled up the sleeves of his brown hooded robe and continued to chop the wood.

Seeing his chance, Harry scurried to the rear of the cottage, crouching down as he ran. He looked at his watch. Three o'clock, the afternoon sun still high in the sky.

Glancing over his shoulder, double checking he had not been spotted, he reached into the tight pockets of his new assassin's uniform and pulled out the master key. As the barrel clicked, Harry turned the doorknob and crept into the cottage, butterflies churning in his gut. Inside, he took a deep breath and tried to relax. The coast was clear. He locked the door and walked softly up the wooden stairs into the main bedroom.

Harry had no idea of the cottage's layout. He knew he would only have a few moments to find a way to complete his contract. But there, right in front of his eyes, was the perfect weapon, almost as though it had been placed there for this very purpose. Above the bed was a large painting encased in a heavy, thick metal frame. The painting had been hung directly above the headboard and pillows. Harry knew immediately it would look like an accident if he sneaked out in the dead of night and cut the cords.

Smiling, he opened the wardrobe door and nestled down in the corner underneath some old, musty fur coats.

CHAPTER 23

The surprise collection….

Hours passed as Harry waited silently in the darkness of the closet. Even though his eyes had adjusted, he could barely make out the time on his watch. The small hand pushed against the six and the long hand neared the ten.

He flexed his calf muscle, feeling the pins and needles burning in his foot, and accidently kicked the side of the wardrobe. It wasn't a loud bang by any means, but in a cottage covered in silence even the slightest knock or bang could be heard.

Seconds later, Harry heard the familiar sound of someone slowly climbing the wooden stairs. He bit his lip and tried to push himself further into the cupboard. His mind played tricks on him in the darkness, each step on the stairs banging like a hammer, echoing through the cottage. Harry could visualise the father monk sneaking up the stairs with a carving knife in his hand. He slowly reached into the side of his boot and pulled out a hidden blade. The blade was shaking in his hand as he tried to make himself breathe slower. *This is what you have been trained for,* he thought. *Pull yourself together.*

As the steps drew closer, wooden floorboards creaked, and the hinges of the doors squealed as one by one the rooms were checked.

Out of nowhere, a sheet of icy purple mist leaked through the tiny gaps in the wardrobe, giving off a sliver of glowing light. The layers of wood on the fine oak doors started to wither and split right in front of Harry's eyes. Tiny maggots crawled through the gaps, falling to the base of the wardrobe with a soft thump.

A clock in the bedroom room chimed for the first time: One. Two. Three. Four. Five. Six.

Six o'clock. Harry gripped the knife tightly, his forearm beginning to shake. He took hold of it with his free hand to try to keep it still. Adrenaline laced his blood, putting him on edge, his breathing too fast, too shallow.

When the doors flung open, he was forced to shut his eyes against the bright light. Fear caused Harry to slash out blindly with his knife. But when he opened his eyes, the monk wasn't there. In his place was the bony, lifeless remains of a human skull wrapped in shreds of black fabric.

For a moment, fear controlled Harry, and he couldn't react. But then his training kicked in and he slashed out again with the three-inch knife, cutting through the ragged robes to where a forearm should have been. As Harry pulled the knife free, he watched in amazement as the shiny new metal slowly lost its colour, then turned to rust and crumbled away.

"Harryyyy Hopkinss," the creature said, his voice a deathly purr.

Harry couldn't move, his mind screaming for him to run, but his legs felt like they'd been cemented in quicksand.

"Who is there?" a voice shouted from the landing. "Reveal yourself!"

The creature broke his gaze from Harry as the door swung open. Lifting his arm, he extended the bony remains of what had once been a finger, and the door slammed shut again, and locked.

Seizing his chance, Harry crawled backwards towards the wardrobe on all fours like a crab.

The creature snarled, and for the first time, Harry noticed a pulsating purple doorway in the corner of the room, a foul green goblin poking her head out. Her long, greasy strands of hair hung over her threadbare cloak.

"Harry Hopkins," the abomination said again. "Your true destiny has not yet been explained to you. Your mother left you with those puny assassins not for them to train you, but to ensure they nurtured your arrogance and selfishness. That band of fools never understood the true power you possess. The power to one day destroy the world."

Reaching out with his spindly fingers, he touched Harry's forehead, offering him a glimpse of the future.

Harry's eyes slowly opened as realisation dawned. In shock, he mumbled, "But how? How do I get such power?"

"You have been selected, Harry Hopkins, along with three others, to release the all-consuming beast, Tyranacus, to purge this earth. Once it is done, you will take your place in the new world. You and your companions will create the new world in your image. Or … you can try your worthless skills against the Brotherhood of Monks." The creature turned and glided to the wall.

"Where are we going?" Harry muttered, dragging himself from the floor to follow, completely transfixed. As he clambered out of the wardrobe, the map to the cottage and the master key clattered to the floor. "Who are you?" he shouted.

"I," the monster roared in an eerie metallic voice, "am the ever eternal. I am the Gatekeeper of life and death, and we are going to begin your training at Elksidian Forest." As the words fell from his bony jaw, wild banshee screams filled the air, vibrating and distorting the walls. "Leave the map and key. I'm sure they will have interesting consequences."

As Harry stepped through into the cold light, the lock on the cottage door opened and the father monk charged into the room.

Looking back from the darkness, the last thing Harry saw was the father monk holding the key and inspecting the map.

"I know all this!" Harry shouted as life returned to his rigid body. He slammed his fists down on the library table. "But what happened? What happened to the Delf?"

The pages flicked over, and the first picture Harry saw was when he'd first arrived at the forest to train, and Lyreco had turned his mouth to rubber, and he'd been unable to speak or breathe. Looking to the next picture, he saw four monks approaching the hidden entrance to the Tribe of Assassins in the church cemetery. Their hands glowed an unnatural pink.

In a gap on the page, below the picture of the monks, a purple square image gradually emerged. As the negative darkened, and the picture slowly unravelled, twelve glowing yellow eyes appeared, and the outline of six fuzzy black figures each wearing the headgear of the assassins. One of them in particular stood out to Harry, the headgear of the High Delf.

As Harry's mind processed the information before him, dozens of likely scenarios came into view, and a voice echoed deep in his mind.

"Yooou had a choice, but you betrayed us. The monks traced the map and key too us, and they destroyed us all. Centuries of work lost in a second, and it is because of you, Harry Hopkins! You shall pay for what you have done to us."

The yellow eyes zoomed into focus on the picture. Harry could see deep into their souls ... deep into the misery and suffering caused to their mortal bodies before the monks turned them into spirits cast to walk the earth for an eternity.

The air flooded into Harry's lungs as he staggered backward, crashing into the shelf and knocking a lamp to the floor. It shattered, casting the library into darkness.

Lies! It's all been lies, Harry thought angrily.

Reaching over, he grabbed the table. "I thought my mother left me with the assassins because she never loved me. But no! It was a trick! The Gatekeeper knew my destiny. He knew the assassins couldn't help me, but they kept me on the path to evil. They needed me to become a Delf, to become a warrior. They didn't care what happened to them. We are all just pawns ... and now they are all gone." He slammed his fists onto the thick wood of the table.

Furious, Harry picked up his book of life and turned it over to the back cover, then slammed it hard on the wooden table. Pausing for a moment, he opened the book from the back to a blank page. He'd just started to turn to the ending when the library door crashed open, illuminating Professor Potts.

CHAPTER 24

The plan unravels….

The first rays of sunshine seeped through the tiny holes in the paper-thin curtains, jabbing and poking at Jimmy's closed eyes. He slowly opened his eyes and let the new day soak into his mind. Rubbing the sleep from the corners of his eyes, he thought back to the crazy events in Lorda's classroom yesterday. The happy, bouncy, carefree teacher had been bound and controlled by whatever twisted magic lay within the mask. Like a drug, he was hooked, his mind poisoned by its evil.

Usually, Jimmy never remembered his dreams, but last night had been different. He recalled the wooden mask floating and circling in his mind's eye. He remembered staring up at the tiny razor-sharp teeth inside the Magworm's rounded mouth as it swallowed him whole. But then it changed. Jimmy had a vague memory of a door closing in the middle of the night from the room directly above his. Harry's room. From that moment on, his dreams had only been about Talula.

Though the details were clouded, he could still feel the warmth as she'd held him. Still feel the fire burning in his stomach when they kissed.

He stared into the mirror, his breath fogging the glass. Wiping away the thin layer of condensation, he stared back at his reflection. His long auburn hair had been dragged over his head, leaving two pieces sticking up like horns at the back. He licked the ends of his fingers and repeatedly tried to flatten the horns, the memory of their kiss still strong in his mind. *Only a dream*, he thought with a sigh.

Jimmy thought back to when he'd returned to the castle the previous day. How Talula had charged from within and flung her arms around him, squeezing him tightly. Almost as though she had been lurking in the doorway, waiting for him to return. He recalled how safe he'd felt in her arms. Like nothing could hurt him.

His chest puffed out with confidence as he ran his fingers through the rest of his hair, trying to give it some volume. *She must feel the same way. After all the things we've been through, all the perilous quests, she must feel the same.*

With one last flick of his hair, he rammed a toothbrush in his mouth and mumbled around it, "It's time to find out once and for all."

Full of excitement, he wiped his mouth with the back of his hand and strode through the bedroom door. As the handle clicked and the door cracked opened, the tiniest seed of doubt began to grow. *But what if she says no?* He closed the door again. "No!" he said, puffing his chest out once more. "I need to know."

Thinking of Talula, Jimmy was sucked through the carpet, landing directly outside the cold, lifeless door with the black, bat-shaped number two. Pausing for a moment, Jimmy took one last deep breath to still the butterflies churning in his stomach.

Gathering his courage, he turned the handle and opened the door. There, staring back at him, draped in her black robes, was Talula. His mouth opened and closed, but like a puppet without a brain, no words came out.

"Jimmy?" Talula said softly, nervously.

Even as a bead of sweat dripped from his head, Jimmy never once broke eye contact, nor did Talula. She finally smiled and reached out to take his hand. The instant their fingers connected, sparks ignited and crackled, and Talula pulled him over the threshold.

As Talula closed her eyes and leant in, her mind suddenly came alive with memories.

That day long ago sat on the tree stump in Elksidian Forest. She could almost feel the unnerving chill slithering down her back as a thick cloud of white air puffed from her lungs. Lyreco had walked through the opening.

'My children,' he'd said, his voice now distant and *muffled. 'Jimmy Threepwood has dared to break our confidence. He's left us all and returned to his family. Without Jimmy, the beast cannot be released, and you will never fulfil your destiny. He must be taught a lesson for his treachery, a lesson that will force him to re-join our family and take his place by our side so that we may one day destroy this world.'*

The memories twisted and altered in her mind. She'd sat for hours with Harry and Percy, trying to come up with a sinister plan, when Percy suddenly leapt from the seat.

'Master, Master,' he had shouted. *'I have it. I have a plan. It's perfect.'*

Percy relayed his plan to them, about the Gatekeeper being sent to Jimmy's school. Talula would plant the seed that the Gatekeeper was planning to kill Will Potts. Percy knew Jimmy would do anything to save his friend. As the Gatekeeper left, Lyreco would have already taken control of Mr Ryding's mind and body, the head teacher. He would convince Jimmy that if the Gatekeeper couldn't kill Will Potts, he would kill his mother.

It had all been a trick, of course. Talula had dressed as the Gatekeeper, creeping into the house where she administered one of her deadly poisons to Jimmy's father. Percy knew that vengeance and fury would consume Jimmy's mind. He would return to the forest to become powerful enough to one day destroy the Gatekeeper. The best part of it all, the Gatekeeper never even knew.

Talula could feel Jimmy's lips coming closer and closer, but all she could think about was Bill Threepwood's lifeless face. His lips slowly turning blue. Suppressed tears and anger swelled within her. She burst into tears, pushing Jimmy back into the passage and slammed the door hard in his face. Afterwards, she reached out with her fingertips and gently stroked the back of the door.

"I'm sorry, Jimmy. I'm so sorry for what I've done to you."

Jimmy walked along the corridor away from Talula's door, bemused by what had just happened. *It felt so right,* he thought, scratching his head. *I just don't understand. Why did she react like that? Have I upset her? Perhaps I should go back. No, no, I need to leave her alone.*

As he went back and forth with his thoughts, replaying the events over and over again in his mind, a high-pitched alarm began to squeal. "Time for class, time for class," it moaned repeatedly. Just as Jimmy placed his hands on his ears, his body went numb and his eyes glazed over. The expensive, thick red carpet distorted below his feet as he was sucked into day two of Lorda's advanced creature conjuration class.

CHAPTER 25

The chalk picture comes to life….

Re-emerging on the other side of the purple, triangular entrance, Jimmy staggered to his feet. He reached out to steady his balance, his fingers touching Talula's hand. "Urm, sorry," he mumbled awkwardly.

Talula just smiled.

Dusting themselves off, the four looked up, astonished to find the classroom in the exact same state as when they'd left it the day before. There was a hole in the far corner of the room where the Magworm had smashed through it. Broken tiles, dust, and rubble littered across the floor mixed with pieces of broken desks and chairs.

Slumped over his desk was Professor Lorda, his ashen skin mixed with a hint of sickly green, and bruised-looking bags beneath bulbous, bloodshot eyes. His head rested in his hands, and he gurgled with each breath.

"Clllaaassss," Lorda groaned, swishing the tassel from his face as he scowled at the cause of all his pain—the wooden mask on his desk. "Class is cancelled today. I'm afraid the effects of the mask have made me … rather ill." Turning away from the class, Professor Lorda muttered under his breath, "No, leave me alone. Look what you did to the classroom. I'm too weak. I cannot put you on again." His fingers crawled uncontrollably towards the mask.

"No," he mumbled again, using his other hand to drag the other back under control. "My students, class is cancelled today." Coughing, he stood wearily, using the wooden desk as support. "However, I have a quest for you. As you may recall, Jimmy's identity ring was, uh, missing. Many years ago, Professor Tinker told me of some things, specifically a plan to destroy the Council of Elders and the world. But he disappeared before I could learn any details.

"Strange things are starting to happen, like Jimmy's missing ring. Only students and teachers can enter the castle, especially the classrooms, so what happened to it. It would appear Professor Tinker may have been right. Today, I received this from a flaming bat." He pulled a folded letter from the mound. Clearing his throat, he read aloud.

My dear old friend, Professor Lorda,

There has been an unfortunate series of events which have led us to where we are now.

I have watched you closely from the shadows. Watched your endless struggle to overcome your addiction to the Scoran Mask. But although you drink from its unlimited pool of power, you use it only to quench your thirst. By letting the mask consume your soul, you could be the most powerful being on Earth.

For now, I leave you with this. The identity ring of Jimmy Threepwood was put in a safe place. It is time to reveal this location and for him to take his identity.

I shall reveal myself to you very soon.

A black, shadowy smudge mark signed the bottom of the page.

Lorda turned the letter over, revealing a roughly sketched charcoal map.

"My students, something is going on here. I must do some urgent research. I need to find Professor Tinker's work. Discover the truth, and quickly, before it's too late. Go. Take the map and the find the ring. There is nothing more you can do here. I must follow the trail. I will tell the elders of the plan once I find out what is going on."

*

The thin paper fluttered in the morning breeze as Jimmy held it by its waxed seal. The red, circular emblem, broken when Professor Lorda opened it, had the indentation of a flower, a rose.

Jimmy scrutinized the poorly sketched charcoal map, his companions following him as they marched through the dark, dank forest. The gnarled and twisted trees bowed over their heads, sucking away the daylight as it cast crooked shadows on the well-trodden path.

Glancing in every direction, Talula, Harry and Percy were certain the lifeless, slender black trees were alive, watching and turning, their eyes following the group's every step. A breeze swept past, disturbing the fallen autumn leaves, whistling and screeching as it rushed past branches and dived through the hollows.

Animals howled in the distance, and ravens squawked high overhead. Talula's anxiety grew at the scuttle of tiny nails digging into the bark to her left. She turned just in time to see a pair of eyes close and fade deep into the darkness.

"Just up ahead," Jimmy shouted, snapping Talula's attention to the front. He pointed deeper into the blackness. Glancing back over her shoulder, Talula could feel something, someone, lurking in the gloom.

Ducking their heads to avoid an overhanging branch, the children stepped through an opening alive with hundreds of tiny yellow eyes, insects scuttling across the floor.

Bringing the letter closer to his face, Jimmy compared the sketch to the layout of the path ahead. On the sketch, a large black X marked the spot. On the dusty path in front of them, one of the trees had been snapped and blocked the road.

"There," Jimmy shouted, pointing under the tree. "Look." He turned to show Percy the letter. "The X on the sketch is under that tree."

As Jimmy took a step closer, a loud, ear-piercing screech came from deep within the paper. He watched as the page flapped uncontrollably in his hand, and a black claw, drawn in a charcoal pencil, swiped across the page, decapitating a tree, that fell, covering the X.

The four companions looked on in wonder as the charcoal drawing showed them standing on a dusty path next to a thin black tree which had fallen across the road. Looking closely, Jimmy could just about make out the two points of the X poking out from under the trunk.

The group crouched into a fighting stance, holding their breath as they prepared for an imminent attack … but nothing happened. The forest remained still, filled only by the scampering of tiny insects, and crickets chirping deep in the brambles.

Jimmy crumpled the letter and shoved it into his cloak. He walked to the fallen tree, running his hands over the newly sliced tree trunk, and a look of dread spread across his face. "It's been slashed apart," he said, looking back at the others.

"Look at these gouges. One of the claws must be as big as my hand."

"What could do this?" Talula asked.

"I don't know," Harry replied, looking all around. "But I bet it was something big, and I'm sure it's not gonna like us. Keep your guard up. Be ready."

"Here," Jimmy shouted, pointing out the jagged tree bark at the point where it had snapped. There, resting on one of the spikey pieces of wood protruding like long, pointed fingers, sat Jimmy's ring. With a quick glance around him, he slid the ring over the wood and held it up to a sliver of light peeking through the trees. He could feel the smooth, cold metal as he rolled it between his fingers. He could feel a tingling as he felt the indentation of the phoenix. But most of all, he could feel the immense, raw power screaming from within the gold, clouding his mind, the ghostly voices commanding Jimmy.

'Feel the power, Jimmy Threepwood! Re-unite us with your bloodline. Merge our powers as was foretold. Once our souls intertwine, your powers will be limitless. Meerrrrge our powers, Jimmy ... merge.'

Without a second thought, with the Gatekeeper's image burned into his mind, he slid the ring onto his finger. The second he pushed the ring over his knuckle, his body spasmed and jerked forward, and he felt his powers drain from his body.

CHAPTER 26

The First….

"This is it," Argon said, shielding his eyes from the midday sun as he looked out at the meadow. "There … look, the old oak tree with the stone pillars either side, just like the drawing." He held up the creased map to compare.

Shimmer stepped off the road and staggered up a shin-high bank overgrown with grass and weeds. Grabbing the cold metal of the farmer's steel gate, he climbed up two of the runs. Shimmer was taken aback as a white horse appeared from out of nowhere and pushed its muzzle into his face, sniffing and nudging. Surprised, he pulled away and lost his grip on the bars, hands clawing the air as he crashed onto the hard road, knocking the wind out of him.

Stratos roared with laughter. "Scared of a horse. Aye, boy, you better toughen up."

"Quiet!" Higuaín shouted, rushing forward. "You'll scare him." The gate bounced under her weight as she climbed to stroke the white stallion's mane. He nuzzled his wet nose into her face. "It's okay, boy," she said, climbing down to tear off a handful of grass. She allowed the horse to graze from her hands.

With a final grunt, the horse trotted off.

Higuaín straddled the gate, then jumped off on the other side. "Come on," she shouted, squelching through a thick patch of mud, almost losing her boot.

Higuaín Del Costa reached the summit of the grassy knoll first. Just as the map had indicated, there stood a giant oak tree in between two stone statues. She pulled off a handful of green moss covering one of the statues. The texture of the moss felt rubbery, like a lump of carpet. The broad statue towered over her, the rough stone base sticking out in back. Four solid wheels were locked in place, two on either side, and a frozen centurion holding a three-pronged trident in its grasp.

"Careful," she said as the others climbed the hill. "Look at these. They're identical. What does the map say about them?"

Argon looked over the map again. Turning it over, he said, "Nothing, it's just a map. There's no writing."

"But where is the sword?" Higuaín asked, circling the statues, looking at the solid stone armour covering its upper body, giving the impression of rippling muscles, and a high crested helmet sitting on its head.

"Try the tree," Shimmer shouted.

Higuaín stepped into the shadow of the ancient oak. The grass felt longer in the shade, almost damp. She circled the tree, finding nothing, just rough bark and branches quivering over her head, bouncing in the breeze.

"There's nothing here," she shouted. "Wait, what's this?" Crouching down, Higuaín fumbled in the long grass, finding an arsenal of discarded rusted knives, swords, and armour.

"What are they, Higuaín?" Argon shouted.

"Old weapons." She turned her attention back to the tree. "Why are they all in this one spot?" she murmured. "Maybe they came from in here?" She plunged her arm into the hollow of the tree.

"Wait!" Argon shouted, a hint of worry in his voice.

"It's okay," Higuaín replied. "I can feel something—" Without warning, a strong hand latched onto her wrist and jerked her into the hole.

"Higuaín!" Stratos and Argon screamed together. Argon reached into the hole but found it empty.

Higuaín plummeted through the darkness, her mind frantic. She fell so fast that the skin on her face rippled and she struggled to breathe. A few seconds later, she slowed, as though caught in a net, and landed gently on a solid wooden floor. The first thing she noticed was the smell of freshly cut pine. The floor under her fingers felt sharp and jagged, woodchips and sawdust shards sticking to her hands. Gathering her senses, she slowly stood, preparing for whatever tried to grab her. Looking around the circular room, she found four tree stumps carefully positioned as seats.

"You have come for the Eden Sword, Higuaín, have you not?" a raspy voice blurted from the shadows, making her jump as she circled on the spot.

"H-how do you know my name?" Higuaín replied.

"My dear girl, we are the trees. We hear everything. Stories, voices, whispers, all passed along by the wind. But you have entered a different kind of tree, as I house the Eden Spire. I am the First." A knee-high wooden sprite morphed out from within the wood. The sprite remained attached to the wall as the tree spoke through it, like a puppet. Higuaín could see the emptiness in its obsidian eyes, partially covered with half an acorn used as a hat.

"Higuaín, many before you have sought the Eden Spire, the only weapon fused with the spirit of Lorratt Del-Vargo. The only weapon capable of killing Tyranacus. But all before you have failed. You will find no ghosts or goblins to defeat here. You must simply survive your friends."

"My friends?" Higuaín asked, puzzled. She glanced around, searching for the sword.

The First laughed. "You see, the elders needed a sophisticated puzzle, something unsolvable. The sword rests in the room ahead, not twenty steps away." The lights leading to the room ignited one by one. As promised, less than twenty steps away, she saw a stone case holding a glistening sword.

"But … your spirit in the outside realm has been twisted and merged with the outer tree. Very shortly, the tree bearing your distorted face will start attacking your friends. The good part is that every time they hit the tree you will face the full force of their attack. They will unknowingly destroy you while at the same time ending their chances of ever killing the beast. Now watch."

Higuaín glanced at the entrance to the room, at the sword almost pleading for her to seize it, but she also saw the vines slithering along the floor, anticipating her to attempt to make a run for it. Although they were only vines, they struck forward viciously, one after another in warning.

A section of bark next to Higuaín slowly peeled off from the inner tree and fell to the floor, revealing a glassy viewpoint. Higuaín glanced out of the corner of her eye towards the sword but thought better about trying to make a run for it. She needed to learn more first.

The First cackled. "Why don't you go for it, my dear, make your move." A further cackle echoed through the hollow room. "The instant you are in range, I assure you, those vines will tear you apart. They have destroyed greater warriors than you."

Just then the viewpoint crackled and hummed, and Higuaín's friends, her companions, filled the screen, prodding and poking at the base of the tree outside. Running towards the glass, Higuaín thumped it as hard as she could. "Argon, help me, I'm in here … Stratos! Dravid!"

"Don't waste your breath; they can't hear you," the First said. "You are lost, and it will be your friends who kill you." The sprite's laugh once again echoed through the passageways.

"Higuaín!" Argon shouted. "Higuaín! Stratos, chop it down. We need to get in there. If we need to, we'll dig up every last root."

Without a moment's thought, Stratos bounded forward, pulling the heavy axe from the sheath on his back. Bobbing the blade handle in his hands, he bent his knees and bounced, lifting the weapon high above his head.

CHAPTER 27

Draconem….

J immy's feet were dragged across the forest floor, his arms draped over the shoulders of Percy and Harry.

When they came to a small clearing, Talula said, "He needs to rest. Look at him!"

"No," Harry replied. "You said it yourself, you could sense someone in the forest. You saw what happened to that tree. Whatever it was slashed the tree in half with one strike. I'm not hanging around here to find out what the creature is or what it wants. We need to get Jimmy away from here. The effects of the ring will wear off soon."

Talula thought back to Lorda's classroom. The voices inside the ring, talking to her, and how she'd felt right after she'd put it on. But Jimmy seemed worse. Whoever had stolen the ring and placed it here had done so for a reason, but deep down inside, she knew Harry was right.

A short time later, the group came to a fork in the road. A tall, rotten wooden signpost had been hammered into the centre. The sign pointing to the left had been smeared in a thick, soggy tar, obscuring the words.

The sign pointing to the right was made of brand-new wood, as though it had never been touched by the elements. Black painted letters showed **Hobnob Forest.** A spindly black arrow pointed to the hollow entrance.

"I don't like it," Percy said, releasing Jimmy's arm from around his neck. With a nod, he signalled Harry to take Jimmy's weight. He walked to the blacked-out sign and wiped his finger across the wet, slimy gunk, revealing the letter e. Pursing his lips, he poked the second sign. It swung on its nail and clattered to the floor.

"This has only just been put on here," Percy said. "The nails are not even rusty, but the workmanship is appalling. Come on." He walked back towards Jimmy's right arm. "I think we should go left. We should take our chances. I've got a really bad feeling about whatever is in there. My gut is telling me not to go that way."

As the group adjusted their bodies to follow the left path, the bushes in front of them shook violently. As they watched, a tornado of twisting sand moved across the road, blocking their path. Within the shifting mass, two pure black eyes flicked open. Then, like rain falling during an April shower, the tiny grains of sand and dust fell to the floor, leaving only a lifeless, shrivelled corpse covered in strands of loose, ripped mummy wrappings. Opening its toothless mouth, it released a silent scream. The piles of sand on the floor leapt up into the air and rotated around the creature's legs.

Pushing the others behind him, Percy faced the creature, warmth snaking from his finger up along his arm. Breaking eye contact, he glanced down and saw his identification ring glowing and pulsating a dark green. As the ring hummed under his skin, he could feel his powers returning. They surged through his cells, sparking his magic back to life. With a mere thought, his eyes ignited in a blaze of fire.

"What are you?" Percy demanded.

Staring at their own rings, hoping their powers would also return, Harry and Talula stood behind Percy, holding up Jimmy.

"Argh, Percy Timmins," the mummy snarled. "The boy hungry for unlimited power. A thirst which can never be quenched, I'm afraid. I thought it might be Harry Hopkins who tried to stand against me first. Nevertheless, I am the pure embodiment of evil. I have risen from my temple in the sands, my place of rest for over two millennia, and I plan to take back what is rightfully mine. The very thing that has also been promised to you. To destroy what is here, then take your place as one of the rulers of the new world. Yes, Percy … I am one of the Children of Tyranacus … companion to Aurabella and Vesty … both of whom you destroyed. But now I have joined forces with my new masters, and we will make sure the elders are punished for what they have done. I, Percy Timmins, am Imjimn-Ra."

"Go!" Percy shouted to the others as a stream of fire blasted from his hands. "Go back the way we came. Go! I'll hold him off."

As Imjimn-Ra casually swatted the intense fire away, tiny sparks landed on his shoulder, sizzling as it burned and melted the moisture-starved wrappings.

Imjimn-Ra turned towards the others, who were scurrying back into the forest. He lifted his free hand, leathery skin squeaking as he curled his fingers into a fist. Instantly, a yellow electrified barrier formed to block the entrance into the forest.

"The other way, quick," Talula shouted, still helping Jimmy, who could barely walk. "Into Hobnob Forest. It's the only way we can go."

After his friends disappeared through the mouth of the woodland, Percy stepped backwards and released his beam of fire into the towering, mummified monstrosity in front of him. He waited a few seconds, then unleashed a second burst.

Once again, Imjimn-Ra simply batted it away.

As the creature took a step forward, Percy was given no choice. Closing his eyes, he relaxed his mind, and morphed into a humongous yellow and blue dragon, roaring and spitting fire into the air. What he didn't expect was for Imjimn-Ra to transform into a raven-black dragon twice the size of Percy's, with piercing, demonic red eyes.

As his impressive wings unfolded, smoke billowed from the nostrils of the enormous black dragon. He opened his mouth to hiss, exposing the fire gurgling in the back of his throat. The fiery glow illuminated the whole of his neck.

Percy growled and swiped forward with his claws in response to the creature's intimidation. Slowly moving from side to side, both dragons sized each other up. The black dragon towered above Percy but was slower in movement and balance.

Seizing his chance, Percy opened his jaws and unleashed a stream of smouldering hot magma.

Imjimn-Ra responded immediately, wrapping his wings around his body like an armoured cocoon. As Percy's blast penetrated deep into the skin, the wings began to glow bright red, and smoke billowed into the air. Refusing to give up, Percy held on with his fiery breath even though his throat screamed in agony. After only a few moments, but longer than he had ever held his fire before, the flame extinguished in a cough and splutter, leaving his throat red and raw.

Imjimn-Ra opened his steaming wings and stood tall, almost grinning, if a dragon could grin. He struck forward with claws, slashing across Percy's face. Blood splattered on the floor.

Percy saw stars as he staggered backwards, collapsing. Imjimn-Ra stood over him on his rear legs, roaring in victory, blasting the sky and covering the treetops in a river of fire. With the last of his strength, Percy tried to unleash another flaming stream, but his throat was too sore and all that came out was a puff of black smoke. Weakened, he morphed back into his human form.

On his knees, Percy waited with bated breath for the dragon to finish him off, but he didn't attack again. He just blocked the path, roaring and grunting in victory.

Not waiting for a further invitation, Percy stumbled to his feet, staggering into Hobnob Forest after his companions.

As Percy staggered away into the woodland, Imjimn-Ra shrank back into his hideous, former human self, smiling as he thought, *You are no match for me. I could have destroyed you all with but a click of my fingers. But no. I must stick to the plan. There are greater forces at work here.*

Reaching behind his back, Imjimn-Ra pulled out a small makeup mirror and clicked the switch as it flicked opened. The glass distorted and wobbled as a black shadowy face appeared.

"Is it done?" the flickering face asked.

"Yes, my Lord Shadow, it is done. Shortly, they will meet the Garn. The plan to rip the children apart from the centre has been put in place. I had some trouble with Percy Timmins, but he was no match for me."

"Fool!" the face roared, startling Imjimn-Ra. "You knew the plan! Did you hurt him?"

"Maybe just a couple scratches across his face."

The black face grimaced. "Do not let it happen again! The second stage of the plan is almost ready. Soon, you and I and our benefactor will take our rightful place on this earth … as its new rulers, and the new children and the elders will be destroyed."

As Imjimn-Ra clicked the mirror shut and walked away, a dollop of the thick tar covering the wooden signpost slipped away. The remaining letters were now easy to make out.

Sepura Castle

CHAPTER 28

The shattered caravan….

"**H**ere!" Harry shouted, panting heavily, his voice slightly raised and filled with panic. "This is far enough. Jimmy can rest here. We need to go back for Percy."

Jimmy groaned as they lowered him gently to the ground. He opened his eyes and reached out helplessly for Talula's arm.

"It'll be okay, Jimmy. Stay here. We won't be long. We have to go; we have to help Percy." As Talula stood, the tops of the trees behind them erupted in a blaze of fire, launching a mushroom cloud of thick smoke into the air.

Talula's stomach sank as she looked up at the smouldering carnage. "Percy!" she shouted. Forgetting about Jimmy, she charged after Harry as they burst back through the shrubbery and undergrowth, swatting aside branches as they ran back towards the curtain of heavy smoke.

Percy screamed out in pain, and Talula pushed on faster, conjuring up all sorts of twisted images in her mind. When she saw Harry's hands ignite in a goblin-green glow, she initiated her own balls of fire. Focused on saving Percy, she didn't notice the tingling green glow spread along her veins. With an involuntary jerk, Talula's body jolted, and her suddenly weak legs caused her to stumble forward a few steps.

Regaining her balance, she looked up just in time to see Percy burst through the trees from the opposite direction and collide head-on with Harry, fear in his eyes. Blood poured from four deep slash marks on his right cheek.

Without taking the time to explain what was going on, Percy scrambled to his feet, his arm reaching out to grip Harry's loose cloak. "Come on!" he screamed. "Move, move, it's coming." He ran towards where they'd left Jimmy.

Glancing over her shoulder, Talula saw Harry holding his ground, his hands glowing with fire, waiting for whoever, or whatever, was following. Talula slowed her pace, noticing the shadow of smoke behind them, but nothing else. Extinguishing his hands, Harry turned and motioned for her to run.

*

Skidding to a stop near Jimmy, Percy turned, waiting for Talula and Harry. Panting heavily, he started taking stock of what had just happened. His right cheek burned as he pressed his hand against the four deep furrows, blood oozing between his fingers.

"You're hurt," came Jimmy's shallow voice from behind, startling Percy. Some of the colour had returned to Jimmy's face. He tore a strip from his sleeve and handed it to Percy for his face. "What happened?"

"Imjimn-Ra," Percy said, his pupils wide as he stared back over his shoulder, tiny beads of sweat clinging to his forehead. His heart thumped painfully in his chest when he heard hurried footsteps crunching through the forest in their direction. Fearing the worst, Percy's muscles tensed as he readied his body, anticipating another fight.

Talula, followed by Harry, pushed into the clearing, the branches flapping in their wake. The only other sound was the scuttling of birds high above their heads.

Sighing, Percy slumped in relief and turned to face his companions, seeing the questions in their faces.

"What was that?" Harry asked, glancing deep into the gloomy forest.

"Look at your face," Talula said, snatching the dirty piece of cloth from his hands and wiping away the streaks of blood.

Percy looked between Talula and Harry, then gently pushed her hand away. "It's another one!" he shouted angrily.

"Another what?" Jimmy asked.

"Another one of the Children of Tyranacus! They're like cockroaches. You kill one and another one appears. A shrivelled mummy … said it was called Imjimn-Ra. Said something about having two masters and destroying us and the elders. What do you think that means?"

"I don't know," Talula said. "But the teachers were terrified of the name 'the Shadow'. Perhaps it has something to do with that. We need to get back to the castle and speak to Professor Potts. There's something strange at play here and we need to find out what, especially with what just happened to us. I mean, why didn't he follow us? He had us beat. Why would he just walk away?"

"He!" Percy shouted. "That thing isn't a he. I don't think it's been a person for centuries. But I'll tell you something, whatever that is, it's by far the most powerful thing I've ever come across."

Jimmy shivered, thinking back to what Madam Shrill had said about an approaching storm, and how scared the teachers were of the Shadow.

"Come on," Harry shouted. "If this is a trap, if there is something worse than Imjimn-Ra waiting up ahead, I for one would rather get on with it. Agreed?"

Each of the companions nodded and followed Harry deeper into Hobnob Forest.

The group pressed on, twitching at every noise in the forest. They remained alert, their eyes flicking in every direction at even the slightest sound. A fine patchy mist had spread across their path, and a mellow breeze swept past the bushes, creating the illusion of whispering voices brought to life by their frightened imagination. Whatever lay ahead on this chilly autumn night, they would be ready.

Turning his head sharply to his left, Jimmy's foot pressed down hard on a dry twig. The snap echoed into the distance, and a hundred birds squawked and flapped away from the overhead trees.

Instinctively, all four companions ducked, looking everywhere for an invisible threat.

Smiling, Harry stood up tall. "Come on! Get a grip, guys. We're acting scared of our own shadows here. We've fought worse than this, and our powers are be—"

"Shhhh," Jimmy hissed, flapping his hand frantically in front of his mouth.

Everyone froze and listened as the wind whistled past their faces.

"There," Jimmy shouted. "Listen."

"Helpp … helpp…" a soft voice echoed towards them, carried on the wind.

"What is that?" Percy said.

"Helpp … helpp…"

"Do you hear it? Come on," Jimmy shouted as he darted off. "It came from this way." Running forward, barely able to see his hands in front of his face, Jimmy headed towards the voice.

"Helpp … helpp meee…"

Suddenly the mist thinned, revealing a well-trodden track in the forest.

"Help!" a female voice shouted from his left.

As Jimmy stopped, the mist parted, as though someone were dragging away a white sheet, revealing a small grassy canyon. Peering down over the edge, he saw where a wooden carriage had veered off the road and smashed into the ground a few feet below, coming to a halt on its side. One of its large wooden wheels continued to spin. Jimmy could see a number of horse tracks and the shredded trail where the carriage had been dragged through the mud after losing control. Further tracks led away from the snapped harnesses, heading into the hollow. The grass below was littered with shards of splintered wood and scattered clothing from the broken suitcases.

"Is there someone there? Help me!" a voice shouted from inside, followed by the repeated banging on the wooden doors.

Without waiting for the others, Jimmy manoeuvred carefully down the bank. His foot slipping, he was forced to run the last bit, then crashed against the bottom of the carriage, causing it to rock back and forth.

"Hang on," Jimmy shouted. "I'll get you out."

Clenching his fist, he conjured a small sparking knife in his hand. Plunging the knife into the carriage, he cut out a door. As the wood fell away, a young girl swooned into his arms. He carried her a short distance from the carnage, her body light as a feather. Jimmy breathed in deep of her fresh aroma, the fragrance reminding him of freshly cut roses. He closed his eyes as warmth ignited in his stomach. Memories surfaced of his father's comforting voice, reminding him of days long since forgotten. Memories of happy times.

The approaching sound of his companions pulled him from his dream. A smile spread across his face as he stared into her perfect, deep blue eyes. "You're Jimmy," he said. "Nice to meet you."

The young girl giggled, twirling his hair, her angelic voice making him shiver when she said, "You're silly. I think you mean you are Jimmy. I'm Daisy. Nice to meet you."

Jimmy's arms refused to let go even as Harry and Percy, followed closely by Talula, stumbled down the bank.

As soon as Harry and Percy caught a glimpse of Daisy, their bodies froze, expressions puzzled.

Percy breathed in deep, her scent opening memories in his mind, like clouds parting to show him a scene. Suddenly, he found himself back in his mansion, soaking into his luxurious carpet as his parents, Anne and Terry Timmins, showered him with gifts and money.

Harry also breathed in her scent but tried to fight off the foreign substance. He gave a glorious fight for a few moments, but Daisy's fragrance melted into his soul, creating the oak scent of Maloy, a potent oil used to polish and sharpen the assassin's weapons. His inner body glowed as he remembered the hours spent locked in the dreary armoury, cleaning, sharpening, and polishing the blades used by the greatest of the Delf.

Daisy pulled a handkerchief from her pocket and reached out to Percy. Smiling, he lunged forward to accept his prize. Before he had time to react, Harry shoved him to the floor and snatched the cotton fabric, lifting it to his nose to inhale the fresh scent.

Percy skidded across the muddy floor, then pushed back to his feet. He clenched his fist, his eyes blinded by rage.

Seeing what was about to happen, Daisy spoke again, and the boys forgot their anger, hanging on her every word. "Please, boys, don't fight." She nudged Jimmy to let her down, which he finally did with some resistance. "What's your name?" she said, wiping the dust from Percy's hair as she studied the deep slash marks on his face.

"Umm," Percy mumbled, never once taking his eyes from her perfectly formed heart-shaped face. "Percy, miss, Percy Timmins."

"And my name is Harry, Harry Hopkins." Taking her hand, Harry kissed her knuckles.

Giggling, Daisy licked her lips. "My name is Daisy De la Terre."

Each of the boys breathed out and smiled, their eyes practically filled with pumping pink hearts.

Talula stood quietly in the background, shaking her head, scorn written across her face. *A girl shows the slightest interest, and they drop everything to help,* she thought, thinking how disappointed she was in Jimmy.

Ahead of her, the boys were making fools of themselves, picking up Daisy's clothes, the suitcases falling clumsily through their faltering hands.

"Daisy," Jimmy said, "your arm, it's cut. Please let me." He grabbed his already torn sleeve.

"No, no!" Percy shouted. He pushed in and dropped the cases he was carrying. "Your cloak is filthy. Let me." He ripped off a strip of fabric and delicately tied it around her arm. Smiling, he sighed, lost in her ocean-filled eyes. "Daisy, would you like to come back to our castle? After all, you need to rest after this ordeal, and we have food, lots of food, and servants."

"Lots of food," Jimmy shouted enthusiastically.

"It would be my pleasure," Daisy said. "Lead the way."

The three boys almost tripped over each other trying to show how many suitcases they could carry. As they struggled up the bank, Daisy turned away, licking her lips. Her tongue morphed into a long, thick black slug as it sucked the moisture from her human skin. *My Master,* she thought to herself, *they are mine.*

As Daisy Del a Terre and the Children of Tyranacus disappeared back into the forest, the smashed wooden carriage rumbled and shook violently before transforming into a hard, yellow shell. A dazed, slimy snail popped its head out and wiggled its antennas, trying to gather its bearings before it slithered under the safety of a log.

CHAPTER 29

The shattered dreams....

Stratos stuck forward with all his might at the base of the tree. In mid-strike, a distorted black face appeared on the crest of the V where the branches joined, its glowing yellow eyes staring straight out. Momentarily distracted, Stratos' axe missed the tree and sliced through the top layer of grass.

Thrashing its branches, the tree struck out, hitting Stratos in the chest, hurtling him through the air. Moaning through its bound mouth, the possessed tree waved its branches like arms, first on its right, then its left.

Either side of the tree, the stones cracked and crumbled around the wheels and hands of the stone centurions, and they pushed free from their concrete prison. Speeding around the ground with tremendous agility on their wheels, the centurions jabbed and poked with their tridents, one of the blades slicing through Shimmer's shoulder.

Argon pushed past one and lunged forward, hitting the shoulders of the other. With an almighty twist of his bare hands, he snapped the stone head clean off. The second centurion drove forward, thrusting his deadly weapon towards Argon's head. Instead, Argon ducked out of the way, and the trident smashed into the chest of the headless guardian, inflicting even more damage on the stone. Argon was thrown to the floor.

The tree groaned as the stone covering the centurion's wrists crumbled away. Gripping the long trident staff firmly in their grasp, both of their wrists rotated like a plane propeller, moving from side to side and then back to the front.

"It's the tree," Stratos shouted as the headless centurion's spinning blade sparked off his axe. "The tree is controlling them. Kill the tree and they'll stop."

Seizing his chance, Shimmer created a lightning bolt in his hands and flung it through the air. The bolt crackled as it glanced off the right-hand side of the thick base, sending a shock wave deep into the bark.

The electrical charge ripped through Higuaín's nervous system, and she collapsed to the floor, holding her rib. Her clothing was singed, and her skin blistered.

"And it begins, Higuaín. Can you get to the Spire before they destroy you?"

She pushed to her feet, fighting against the burning pain. Hot metal seared a line across her shoulder, then her thigh, sending her crashing into the wall. But even through the excruciating pain, she managed to keep her eye firmly locked on the weapon.

The First laughed. "It's no use, Higuaín. You can never win. I've seen this battle many times before. Warriors come in numbers to retrieve the sword, but once the tree starts attacking them, they always end up destroying it. Unfortunately, they also kill the person on the inside. It became a little boring, you know, over too quickly, so I introduced the stone guards … to add a bit of fun. But they are weak, not much of a challenge."

Higuaín pushed away from the wall, using her momentum to fall forward a few steps. She crept on with an outstretched arm as a fireball exploded into her back, sending her smashing face-first onto the floor. Writhing in agony, she dug her nails into the hard wood and began to drag herself forward.

Stratos charged forward, ducking the fierce flailing of the tree's left branch. Diving through the air, he sliced a chunk out of its right branch and then landed in a forward roll. The tree screamed, thrashing out, catching Stratos as he stood. The connection hit hard, sending him rolling down the side of the bank.

Dravid watched from a short distance away as the tree dragged its roots from the earth and slowly turned to finish Stratos off. Dravid ran to help his injured companion. As the tree lumbered forward, Dravid pulled a knife from Stratos' belt and threw it as hard as he could, the blade stuck to the hilt in the wood.

Argon generated a fireball and threw it at the headless centurion. As the scorching ball hurtled through the air, it hit the stone warrior full in the chest, obliterating half of its upper body, showering the air with falling shrapnel. At the same time, Shimmer created a sizzling lightning sword, slicing through the back portion of its body.

The front two wheels continued driving forward, but without the stability of the back half, the centurion fell to the floor, its spinning trident churning into the mud. With a final slash, Shimmer cut the warrior in two.

"Stratos!" Argon shouted as the centurion crumbled. When the tree chewed through the ground towards his companion, he created a fireball and launched it against the bark of the tree. The tree groaned, its bark left black and smouldering.

When his ball of fire hit the tree, Dravid had felt something … something lost, and far, far away. Closing his eyes to mediate, his spirit soaked into the ground. Images travelled through the ancient tree like passages, turning and moving. Around one corner, he saw her. "Higuaín…?"

Jerked back to the fight, Dravid saw Argon unleash a second and third fireball, igniting the branches. Portions of the solid bark were glowing fiery red now. As Argon raised his flaming hands again, Dravid shouted, "Argon! Noooo! Stooooop! It's Higuaín!"

Higuaín's clothes smouldered as smoke filled the air, making it hard to breathe. The last two fireballs had bubbled her flesh, and yet she still clawed herself forward.

A sinister, hollow laugh filled the tree. "This is it, Higuaín. You finally meet your end. One last hit, that's all your body can take, and once again, the puzzle wins."

Higuaín didn't try to look back. She just closed her eyes and clawed her way forward.

Too late. Argon didn't hear Dravid's scream until after he'd thrown the projectile. It blazed through the air in slow motion, free-falling like a comet.

Shimmer had just plunged his lightning sword into the last centurions head when he heard Dravid's yell. With no time to think or aim, he threw the sword through the air. Holding his breath, he knew everything hung in the balance. Higuaín's life now hung in the hands of fate.

As though guided by magic, the lightning bolt moved seamlessly through the air, spearing the fireball. Both detonated in a shower of sparks in mid-air.

Shimmer let out the longest breath as he looked up thankfully to the heavens.

Higuaín braced for the final impact, but it never came. She knew then she'd been saved. Knew her companions, her friends, had realised it was her. The First's tension and anxiety washed over her like an ocean wave, invigorating, as though she had been given a new lease of life, new hope.

"What is going on!" the First screamed through the animated tree sprite. "This can't be! No!"

Higuaín sighed, her body raw, like a thousand hot pokers were being pushed deep into her skin.

Crawling on her hands and knees, she reached the stone steps and used them for support as she slowly climbed. Reaching forward, she grabbed the enchanted Spire and pulled it from its resting place, holding it aloft in victory. *I've done it! I've retrieved the sword needed to kill Tyranacus.*

At her touch, the mystical weapon came to life. Higuaín stared in wonder at the solid gold handle leading to the circular shaft. Three smoky blades poked out the end, encased in some form of glass.

Turning back towards the First, Higuaín's strength finally left her. Her legs gave out and she collapsed. The Eden Spire slipped from her hand, bouncing once, twice, down the steps. Higuaín could do nothing but watch as it bounced, her heart in her mouth. The words Argon had read from the note reverberated through her mind like a pinball,

'Eden Spire is the most fragile blade on the earth and could shatter with the faintest touch.'

Noooo! she screamed in her mind. The Spire clipped the bottom step, one of the blades exploding. Shards of shattered glass spread across the floor as the shifting black substance encased within the blade seeped into the wood, lost forever.

Higuaín pressed her forehead to the cold floor as the First spoke, not with mocking laughter this time, but defeat.

"Higuaín Del Costa, against all odds you have beaten the puzzle. Not only did your friends discover what was happening to you, but you battled on with the gravest of injuries. Your battle has won you the Elder Spire, and a chance to one day destroy the beast and save this world … but mark my words, Higuaín, do not trust everyone. Not all can be taken at face value."

With the last of her blurred vision, she saw hundreds of green vines cocoon her body, and felt her pain being drained away.

Time slowed as she reached out with her battered fingers, but no matter how hard she tried, the mystical weapon remained just out of reach. With one final lunge, she fell forward. The Spire and stairs melted away. She screamed in her mind as she fell through the empty black space, her weightless body carried by an invisible force. Moments later, she was set gently on the soft grass.

"Higuaín, Higuaín, she's hurt!" a voice shouted. "Get those vines off her! Get them off!"

The voice became crisper, and she recognized Argon. As the air flooded back into her lungs, her eyes snapped open.

"You're okay," Argon said in relief, running his hands over her body, looking for injuries, but there weren't any. Her clothing was singed and shredded, but her skin was fresh and vibrant.

"The Spire," she mumbled weakly. "Where is the Spire?"

"Here it is," Dravid shouted, picking it up. The blade radiated in the sunlight. With a mere touch, the Spire came alive, raising his hair as it hummed along his arm. Dravid ran his thumb carefully over two buttons on the handle, one above the other. The top one, just out of reach of his fingers, was red. *Placed intentionally out of the way to prevent it accidently being pressed,* he thought. The blue one sat snuggly under his grip. The inky blank substance mesmerised Dravid as it wiggled inside the glass case. He thought about pressing the buttons but didn't dare.

"Hold down the blue one," Higuaín said, sitting up.

"How do you know what will happen?" Shimmer asked, staring.

"It spoke to me. It told me how it works."

Without a second invitation, Dravid held down the blue button. The rounded shaft spun violently, spun like a carousel, sending a wave of vibration along Dravid's hand and into his arm. The power, the energy, soaked into him.

"It's like a gun," Higuaín shouted above the noise. "It will fire a blade if you press the red button. Hopefully, we strike deep into Tyranacus' heart." She sighed, staring at where the third blade should have been, only a nub of glass left. "One blade is destroyed. There are only two chances left." She looked shamefully at the floor. "We'll have to make sure those two are enough. There will be no more chances."

CHAPTER 30

The silver salt pot….

Daisy Del a Terre peered through the window, staring out over the vast gardens of Sepura Castle. She rested her shoulder against the cold stone walls in her damp, rarely visited room near the top wing of the castle, a faint smile curling the edges of her mouth. Majordomo had lit the kindling in the fireplace and the torches hung on the walls, but Daisy preferred the gloom and the moist, humid air. It was the closest she would get to her normal environment. She'd extinguished the crackling flames before taking her place against the open window.

A full silvery moon hung high in the air, casting its rays over the window. Her human skin faded under the moonlight, allowing her true Garn form to emerge, her slimy grey skin almost glowing. She ran her slippery fingers over her lips, her black, greasy hair clinging to her face. A puddle of sticky yellow slime formed on the stone floor beneath her feet. As she walked to the second window, the trail of sludge followed her every step.

Licking her lips with her black tongue, the Garn scratched frantically behind her ear like a flea-bitten dog. "I hate this human skin." She scowled, scratching away tiny flecks of dead skin that rained down to the floor. "I'll be glad when the children are dead, and I can go back home. Arghh," she groaned, scratching again, leaving four red nail marks along her skin.

It was just so dry. She hated it, like wearing a fur coat all day. Furious, the Garn turned, thrust her back against the jagged corner of the windowsill and scratched her back up and down like a bear on a honey tree. A patch of slime dribbled down the wall and pooled on the floor.

"I need to make this quick," the Garn said. "Those stupid boys will do anything for me, even kill each other." The cracked edges of her lips turned up at the thought. "I will get through tonight and then make subtle suggestions tomorrow. It will only take a few whispers in their ear. They won't even know what they're fighting each other about."

As she walked back to the first window, the light of the moon was temporarily blocked by the wall, and her vile, putrid skin changed back to the soft, silky skin of Daisy De la Terre.

The wooden door shook as someone knocked hard three times, breaking the Garn's sinister thoughts. She held her breath, smirking at the faint squabbles going on outside the door.

"We agreed I would knock, and you would speak to her."

"No, we didn't. You decided that, Harry. Like everything else, you go first, not giving a moment's thought to anyone else."

"Hey! That isn't fair."

Stepping back into the darkness, the Garn allowed her human form to fully disguise her true identity. Blinking once, the fireplace and torches burst back into life.

As the hinges of the door creaked open, sending a squeal down the spiralling staircase, the three boys stood to attention.

"Daisy," two of the boys said at once before giving each other a filthy stare.

"Dinner is ready," Jimmy said.

"Oh, please come in and w—". Daisy stopped, noticing the large puddle of slime glistening on the floor. Pushing the door almost closed, she peered through the small crack. "A lady needs time to prepare. Would you mind waiting outside for a few moments while I, urm, change my dress. Yes, change my dress." Without a further word or complaint, Daisy slammed the door in their faces.

The walk down the long, narrow passage to dinner was filled only by the clanking of Majordomo's metal talons striking the chequered marble floor. With every step, he groaned as air leaked out of his rotten lungs.

Daisy Del a Terre studied every precious painting and artefact decorating the walls. Like a girl in a sweet shop, she marvelled at the treasures hidden from the rest of the world since the beginning of time.

The portrait of King Rasbar she thought to herself, *the forgotten headless King*. The voice in her mind said the name perfectly in the lost language. A language a normal human couldn't pronounce without breaking their jaw and pulling it forward two inches. *The Last Vase of Mauritius, holding the remains of Dejjagger, the sword maker.* She turned to read the engraved golden plaque. Since the beginning of time, the Garn had lurked in the damp shadows of the world, watching, waiting, only serving those who summoned her, and only then if they were truly worthy of her power. Trinkets such as these meant nothing to her, but it was worth noting where they rested. Information could be useful to future clients. Her eyes noted a few more of the treasures as she sucked her bottom lip.

The three boys watched her every movement as she glided effortlessly along the floor. Daisy's invisible scent put a firm leash around their necks, pulling them obediently along.

Majordomo pushed open the heavy oak doors leading to the grand dining hall. Clearing the cobwebs from their minds, the three boys strode ahead of Daisy and Talula and stepped into the darkness.

"You are late," an icy voice said, startling Jimmy.

A click of fingers echoed in the room as it exploded into light.

"Professor Potts," Jimmy said, puzzled. "We apologise. We had to collect Daisy. Why are you sat in the dark?"

Professor Potts turned his head from the centre and looked with disgust at the three boys. "I've been feeling unwell these past few days. Something is pulling at my mind, and I needed time to reflect on it. But for now, we have a guest." He stood from his place at the head of the table and gestured for Daisy to take her seat of honour next to him.

Barging past Talula, Jimmy took a seat opposite Daisy. He noticed Professor Potts' face looked ashen and sweat dripped down his cheek. His forehead creased with worry, Professor Potts gripped Jimmy's hand firmly, his palm moist and sweaty. The ruby crystal hanging around his neck clouded as the face of Jimmy's old school friend Will Potts pushed through the reflection.

Furious at being shoved out of the way, Talula took a seat and gave Jimmy a firm elbow to his ribs. He coughed, and when he looked back at the crystal, the image had faded. He forgot about it as Daisy's sweet aroma took hold once again.

"Ladies and gentlemen," announced the professor, who seemed to have regained his composure. "Let the food flow." As the words left his mouth, the candles on the long wooden table flickered to life with a blue flame. Gleaming cutlery sparkled on the table as wine glasses filled from the bottom with rosy red Tree-salt wine. Soft melodies from floating, eloquent stringed instruments filled the air.

As the group basked in the music, lost in the heavenly strums, a tiny chime rung inside a dumb waiter set within the wall. Sliding up the hatch, Majordomo nodded at whatever lurked inside. Hoisting a large black tray on his shoulder, he carried it towards the table. He handed them all a covered bowl, serving the guest first, then Talula.

As Talula and Daisy lifted their covers, their expressions clearly told different stories.

"What is this?" Talula said, horrified as bubbles surfaced and popped in the thick green sludge, eight shiny black insect legs poking out. She groaned, scrunching her face up as she grabbed her mouth.

Majordomo stopped and wheezed, "It's Ickleback soup, my Master. "A delicacy from our very own gardens."

Daisy meanwhile was delighted. The Ickleback bug was rare and succulent. She had spent hours, days even, searching for just one. Slurping the soup, she savoured the warm crunchy texture.

Majordomo circled the long table, the bottom half of which was empty, and approached and refilled her bowl with a second helping. Daisy released her corruptive scent which snaked through the air. Majordomo coughed and spluttered at the invisible smell, pushing it out through the holes in his cheeks and chest.

Daisy groaned softly and slurped her soup, splashing it all over her mouth.

Talula shook her head as she watched Daisy, the girl on the verge of licking her bowl clean. She found Harry pushing the black insect around his plate. Deciding to give it a try, Talula asked Daisy to pass the salt. The air became thick with an awkward silence as Daisy ignored her.

"I'll get it," Percy said. He reached over a dessert spoon and through two wine glasses, his fingertips poking the salt cellar. The metal pot fell onto the table, the tiny grains of salt forming a small mound.

The instant the pot landed, Daisy sprang up from her seat. She jumped backwards like a scared cat, knocking her chair to the floor, her wide eyes locked on the small white pile of salt.

"Daisy?" Jimmy said.

"What is it?" Harry asked.

Not once looking away from the mound on the table, Daisy replied with a quaint giggle, "Oh, nothing. I just didn't want to ruin my new dress. Percy, would you be a dear and clean that up? If I get that on my dress, it will just ruin it."

There, stood in front of the window, illuminated by the silvery light of the moon, Talula could see it. Daisy's skin faded away, leaving a slimy grey coating, her raven hair covered in grease and stuck to her face. Her purple lips were cracked and blistered, her eyes hollow and empty.

"I knew it," Talula mumbled, ready to pounce. She glanced at Harry sitting next to her, staring at Daisy, but his expression didn't change. "Can't you see her," Talula asked impatiently.

"Yeah," Harry replied, barely listening. "Isn't she beautiful?"

"What?" Talula whispered. "What has she done to you?"

In the midst of the commotion, Jimmy once again felt a firm grip on his right arm. Looking at Professor Potts, he saw his face had altered. The tired, sweaty blue skin had faded, leaving the fresh face of a boy no older than seventeen.

"Jimmy," the boy said, his voice soft and clean, no longer filled with the grit and torment of the world. "I don't have long. It's me, Will. Help me, Jimmy. He has me trapped. My soul, it's being controlled by the necklace. The necklace." The grip on Jimmy's shoulder tightened. Professor Potts shook his head and his skin once again turned battered and worn.

You're still in there! Jimmy thought. *Don't worry, Will, I'll get you. I'll save you if it's the last thing I ever do.*

CHAPTER 31

Blinded by desire....

Pulling the cowl of her cloak over her head, Talula crept up the stone steps. Heart thumping strongly in her chest, afraid of being caught, she kept to the shadows, able to hear Daisy walking ahead in the distance, her footsteps echoing through the empty passage.

When Daisy's footsteps slowed, Talula dived out of sight behind a pillar, holding her breath. She could feel Daisy's eyes scrutinising the darkness. In what seemed like an eternity, the footsteps resumed, walking in the opposite direction. Blowing softly as she released her held breath, Talula counted to ten and skulked after her again. She poked her head around the corner just in time to see Daisy close the door to her bedroom.

Crouching down, Talula tiptoed to the door and pressed her eye against the keyhole. Daisy strode across the room, lit up only by the sliver of moonlight. When she turned to face the door, Talula jerked away, even though she knew there was no possible way Daisy could see through the keyhole.

"Argghhh," she could hear Daisy shouting angrily, followed by a violent scratching sound. "That stuff! Urgh, I can taste that vile stuff. It's all over me! I can smell it everywhere." She kicked a wooden chair which scraped across the floor and crashed into the wall.

"I can't take it anymore. This skin, I need to get out of it."

Talula looked back through the keyhole, her mouth dropping open in shock as the beautiful and perfect Daisy Del a Terre slowly shrivelled and hunched over. Her slimy raven hair hung over a sickly grey gaunt face, her dirty brown nightgown clinging to her bony frame. A puddle of grey sludge formed around her feet, the stench of which floated under the door, gagging Talula.

Holding her mouth, Talula couldn't believe what she was seeing. How could this revolting creature have the boys falling all over themselves to please?

"What are you?" she whispered.

Talula watched on as the creature stretched her arms high above her head, almost as though she had just risen from bed.

"That's better," the creature said. She coughed, sending a clear substance splattering on the wall. "Those sickening, horrid humans touching me, falling all over themselves for me." Her body quivered in disgust.

As anger swelled deep inside, Talula charged her hands.

"Tomorrow," the Garn shouted. "They will do my bidding, and they will all die!"

Talula snapped. Her hands sparking with green energy, she reached out and gripped the door handle firmly. The door exploded, launching tiny shards of wood across the room like tiny knives.

The Garn snarled as Talula bounded into the room, her hands a blur of blazing emerald light. Ducking and weaving from the rage filled strikes, the Garn waited for the exact moment to strike, sending out streams of stringy white gunk from her every pore. The sticky substance entangled around Talula, pushing her hard into the wooden bed post. She raised her right hand, finding it completely cocooned in the white sludge. The creature stared at her with empty, hollow eyes as she struggled to break free of the stinky substance.

"What are you?" Talula groaned. "What do you want?"

Tilting her head to one side, the creature licked her lips and pressed close to Talula's cheek, whispering, "I am the Garn! The hint was in the name, Daisy Del a Terre or in some languages, Daisy of the earth. I have been summoned to end your reign of terror. You are too powerful to beat as a group, so my new master decided to fracture you from within. What a great plan, don't you think? The boys fall in love with me, and with but a hint of persuasion, destroy themselves to be with me. If only they could see my true form."

"Don't you worry about that," Talula shouted defiantly, "They'll see who you are! I'll make sure of that. They'll see what you've done! Help! Jimmy! Harry! Percy!"

With an aggressive wave of the hand, a fist-sized ball of snot splattered over Talula's mouth. The Garn stepped back as footsteps charged up the passage. Three concerned faces clambered over the door and ran to the middle of the room. The three boys stared at the Garn and then directly at Talula, who was strapped to the bed post.

Relieved, Talula knew they would finally see the real Daisy, the creature, the Garn, for what she really was. They would destroy her.

The three boys paused, surveying the room, their gazes flickering between the bed post and Daisy. Percy finally said, "Daisy, are you okay? What happened to the door?"

Talula couldn't believe her ears. They couldn't see her. Mumbling, she rocked the bed post as she tried to force open her mouth through the gunk.

"I'm okay, boys," the Garn said. She ran her fingers through Talula's hair as she walked past, "It was a gust of wind. It blew the door off its hinges."

"Really," Jimmy said. His eyes glazed over, only able to see the cloak of beauty covering her vile skin. "I can't feel any draft, but as long as you're alright."

"I'll come back first thing in the morning," Harry said, pulling Percy and Jimmy out of the room. "I'll come back and fix the door."

The Garn smiled and watched as the boys walked down the passage. She paused for a moment, smirking as they started to squabble. "You see, Talula Airheart, there is nothing you or anyone else can do. I'm untouchable, impervious to your mortal weapons. Nothing can harm me. Your friends are so blinded by their love for me. They barely notice anything else." Clenching her fist into a ball, the white sludge hardened and shattered into a thousand pieces, Talula dropping to the floor as it released her.

"Now leave! And be ready tomorrow to watch your friends die. It may be more interesting to get them to turn on you first. Now that is an idea."

Talula didn't waste any time. Scrambling to her feet, she watched the lines of moonlight glowing over Daisy's skin as she ran towards the open doorway, staggering over the crumpled pieces of shattered wood.

CHAPTER 32

A trip into the darkness....

Talula grew lightheaded as she charged frantically through the halls, her breathing far too rapid, her eyes filled with tears, Turning a corner, her legs turned to jelly and she crashed face-first into the wall. Desperate, she pressed her back against the wall and waited for the creature to follow, but she never did. Hysterical, she sat on the floor and rocked back and forth, unable to calm down.

What can I do to stop this monster?

Holding her breath, Talula pressed her hand against her heaving chest and thought about her room with the black bat emblem on the door. Slowly, she sank into the floor.

*

Majordomo had heard the commotion and raised voices in the bedroom. Approaching Daisy's room, he peered around the corner just in time to see the feathered ends of Talula's hair sink into the carpet. He paused for a moment, listening. In the distance, he heard Percy talking to the others.

"What was all that about?" Percy said. "I could swear I heard Talula shouting for us from Daisy's room, but she wasn't even there."

"Maybe we should go look for her," Harry said.

There was a short pause, then Jimmy said, "Daisy said she would be fine. We'll see Talula in class tomorrow. I'm not worried. She's been acting weird ever since Daisy arrived. Maybe she's jealous."

"She has been acting very strange," Percy replied, "and did you see Daisy's door? It was completely obliterated. Do you think the wind really did that?"

"That's what she said," Harry murmured, looking back over his shoulder.

Majordomo lurked in the shadows as eventually the three bedroom doors all closed at the same time. He could see the shadows beneath their doors, as if they were waiting to see if the others tried to leave again. *Strange,* he thought. *I've never heard Jimmy talk about Talula so coldly. Come to think about it, they've all been acting very strangely.* As he turned back to where Talula had been, he saw a tiny trickle of blood on the wall and the carpet.

Sinking through the floor, he landed outside of Talula's room. The door was ajar, and a beam of light spread into the hallway. Approaching the door, he could hear Talula weeping inside. Gently tapping the door, he heard the quick panic of movement as Talula's voice shouted out, "Who is it?"

Majordomo pushed the door open, aware by her expression that he was not who she'd been hoping to see. She sniffled, straightening her cloak, her puffy eyes pink from tears.

"Mistress Talula," he wheezed, "is everything okay?"

Talula stared back at him for a few moments before sitting down on the edge of the bed. She pushed her head into her hands as she said, "It's too late." She groaned. "It's over and there is nothing anyone can do."

"What's over?" Majordomo asked.

"Everything," she said, lifting her head up. "That thing … Daisy, it's all an act. She isn't a girl. She a creature, a slimy monster who has some sort of control over the boys. They are falling all over themselves for her. I tried to stop her, but she took everything I threw at her. Even though she revealed her true form, the boys couldn't see it. She could have killed me then. She had me trapped, but she let me go. By tomorrow, she will have turned the boys against me, then she'll have them destroy each other."

"But why," Majordomo asked. "What can she gain by this?"

"I don't know. She mentioned a master, someone who has brought her to this world to fracture us from within. She said she was the Garn."

"The Garn," Majordomo said thoughtfully, the flaps of his skin moving as the air passed out through the holes in his cheeks. "Hmmm, and she's working for a master." He groaned, closing his eyes. "The Garn … that name is familiar for some reason. Something about a creature taking a human form. There's something you should see. Something that may help us."

Majordomo helped Talula stand. Sinking through the floor, they surfaced on the landing outside the two solid oak doors with a sign which read **Armory**.

Walking to the centre of the hallway, Majordomo stopped in front of a large red tapestry hung by a golden nail hammered into the wall. "Which one was it," he repeated as he stopped in front of six other similar tapestries. He walked back to Talula, motioning her forward. "I think this one is it."

Talula stared at the grand maroon tapestry covering a large portion of the wall. It depicted a series of grey stone steps descending into darkness. She gritted her teeth as she ran her fingers over the coarse surface. "What is it?"

"You'll see." He took her hand. With a giant lunge, he stepped into the hanging tapestry, dragging Talula with him.

The air became thick, like a woolly jumper had been pulled over her head, and Talula began to panic. It was boiling hot and as she struggled to breathe, tiny bobbles of fluff leapt into her mouth, tickling down her throat.

With a final stumble, they landed in a square courtyard, and Talula was finally able to suck in a lungful of clean air. Glancing behind her, she found the tapestry now depicted a series of steps climbing back up into darkness. Curious, she grabbed the paper-thin fabric and swung it forward, finding only a solid stone wall behind it.

"This way," Majordomo said.

A wooden door creaked open, then slammed shut behind them as they walked along a narrow passage. The moist air was stale, far from being fresh. At the end of the passage was a cell door, everything beyond it lost in darkness.

"What is this?" Talula asked, starting to feel uneasy. She readied the green spark in her hands.

"This may be able to help us," Majordomo spluttered, "though it has never spoken a word in thousands of years."

Talula stared into the shadows and, as her eyes slowly adjusted, she saw a wooden bed hanging by chains from the wall, and a pungent brown toilet surrounded by flies. She narrowed her eyes, seeing a pile of yellow sludge on the floor. In the middle floated something small and black. Looking back at Majordomo, she raised her eyebrows in question.

Talula jumped as a wild creature pounced from within the sludge, transforming in mid-flight. Before she could react, the lightning-fast creature soared through the air and clamped its claws around Talula's throat.

CHAPTER 33

The most powerful mystic to walk the earth….

T he creature screamed in Talula's face, saliva dripping from its fangs.

Majordomo lunged forward and grabbed its wrists, trying to pry open its claws. With her windpipe being crushed, Talula watched in horror as a faint gas snaked from the creature's skin and floated around Majordomo's neck and up into his nose.

"Release your grip," the creature hissed at him, then spat a black inky substance on Talula's face. "Release your hold and open the cell door." The creature looked perplexed when Majordomo didn't respond, but the distraction was all Talula needed. Igniting her hands, the mild explosion threw Talula backwards into the corridor. The creature was thrown hard into the wall at the rear of its cell.

Majordomo clambered to help Talula stand. "Your lungs, they are damaged," she gasped, winded. "I saw it. She released a gas which tried to slither into your body, but it leaked out of the scars. That's how it was trying to control you. That's how it controls the others. It's a Garn. How did you catch it?"

"It's been locked away here for thousands of years. It took control of one of the first children. When you were telling me about the way the other three boys were reacting to her, it rang a bell, but I couldn't quite remember."

"How did they defeat it? How did they lock it in here," she asked impatiently?

"They didn't defeat me!" the creature hissed. "They tricked me into this prison. I told them it wouldn't hold me forever, and it seems I was right."

"What are you?" Talula asked.

"I am the Garn. You foul creatures disturbed my sleep thousands of years ago. You tried to control me, but you must first ask for my help before I will agree to call you master. I took control of your ancestors like puppets, but my plan was foiled."

"How did they stop you," Talula said, grabbing the gate.

"Now that would be telling, wouldn't it? It is clear one of my sisters is controlling your friends." She licked her lips with her black, slimy tongue. Talula studied her dry, cracking complexion. *The first Garn is greasy and covered in slime.*

"This prison," Talula said, "it only releases a small amount of moisture into the air. Just enough to keep you alive, but weak. Help us and I will increase the quantity. I can make this comfortable for you. Tell us how to stop your sister."

"Stop my sister!" the creature shouted, lunging forward to grab the metal bars, staring daggers at Talula. "It would take more than an offer of moisture and comfort to betray a sibling."

"What will it take then? What do you want? Freedom?"

"After all this time, freedom is no good to me. I live only for vengeance. Do you happen to carry vengeance with you?"

"Vengeance?" Talula asked. "How can I carry that?"

The Garn smiled. "I do not know how to kill a Garn … though I know someone who may have the information you seek, but you must first promise to return to me with a trinket? It is nothing more than an instrument for parlour tricks?"

"What is it," Majordomo asked.

"First promise to return the item to me and sign the deal in blood. Afterwards, I will reveal how to fulfil your quest."

Talula looked at Majordomo and then the grinning prisoner. She had no idea what this item was, but what harm could it cause if it helped keep her friends from being killed. *Anyway, when I find the secret, I will destroy this one too.*

Talula wiped blood from the inside of her cheek from her earlier fall and then held her palm out in front of her. The Garn smiled, exposing her long fangs. Nicking the top of her finger with her teeth, she smeared the yellow ooze onto her palm and sealed the deal with a handshake.

As Talula looked at her palm, her blood and the yellow ooze hissed and bubbled, burning a black ring into her skin. A small black arrow grew in the centre with its head poking through the circle.

"That is the deal ring," the creature said. "Fail to honour our deal and your soul becomes my possession. Far to the east is the person you seek." The black circle on her hand spun around as the arrow bobbed about from side to side like a compass, then locked in the two o'clock position.

"There lies the most powerful mystic to ever walk the earth, the almighty Golion Gerwagg, and he will reveal the secret of the Garn. But, in his possession will be the *Sight of Passing*. This is the item I wish for you to collect." As the words fell from her tongue, the dial on Talula's hand turned bright red. "Talula Airheart," the creature hissed. "The deal is now set."

*

Wind streamed past Talula's wings as she soared high into the night. Gliding through the clouds, the dial on her hand ignited a flaming red and spun around, clicking and grinding. In an instant, Talula felt as though the air got sucked out from under her. She received an almighty shove from behind by an invisible force, knocking the wind out of her, and she began to fall. As the ground rocketed towards her, time suddenly slowed. In mid-air, and against her will, she morphed back into human form and crashed, skidding along the floor. As she looked back, she could see the shadow form of her bat floating through the air behind her.

With the echo of clicking fingers, the night sky darkened, becoming pitch black out, almost as though someone had turned out the lights. Peering up, she found the stars gone, barely able to see by the faded light of the moon. An icy breath of wind gave her a chill, and she blinked and rubbed her eyes, desperate to make them adjust to the poor lighting.

"Come to see the all-powerful, have you?" a chilling voice whispered from behind her.

A second voice muttered down the back of her neck, "He is expecting you. He can see everything."

"Golion Gerwagg!" Talula shouted into the shadows. "I come to ask a question of the all-powerful mystic. Will you grant me an audience?"

"Grant me an audience, grant me an audience, grant me an audience," was echoed by the voices.

Talula shuddered, feeling an invisible hand stroking her hair, or was it only her mind playing tricks. Her right palm sparked, creating a green fireball, illuminating the area before it suddenly changed to black and fizzled out. She tried again and again but found her magic had been drained.

While distracted by her hand, something shoved her, and she stumbled forward. Planting her feet firmly into the floor, she was pushed again and again by multiple hands through the darkness. Suddenly, bright lights and the loud music of a fairground burst into life, startling Talula.

To her right, the dodgem cars sped around, crashing into one another. She ducked as a rollercoaster thundered through the air over her head. Talula frowned, taking short steps forward. The fair was a living ghost town, plenty of clanking metal and joyful music, but no people. To her left, the life-sized wolfman screamed outside the ghost house as a giant skull chuckled maniacally, its laser red eyes following her every movement.

Seagulls squawked, flapping their wings as she walked along the boardwalk, and the unmistakable smell of chips wafted across the sea front. Looking ahead, she saw rows and rows of arcade video machines. As she took two steps forward, the dial on her palm glowed bright red again, then faded.

She stopped in front of a tall glass case. Inside was a poorly made wooden puppet tied together with wires. The puppet had a painted beard and flopped about every now and then, doing a little jiggle.

What's this? Talula thought, shaking her head. In the distance, a big Ferris wheel caught her attention as it rotated slowly, though she couldn't see if anyone sat in any of the carriages. Hearing a whirling alarm, she turned her attention back to the wooden puppet.

"Where is he then?" she whispered. "Where are you?"

The puppet rattled once, making a high-pitched screeching noise followed by a series of flashing lights. The lights flashed on one by one, leading her eyes downward to a slot and a sign which read: **Only £1 for a question answered.**

"Question answered," Talula murmured.

The machine sprang into life: *Ding, ding, ding, ding!* as a neon light pinged on. **£1 a question for the all-powerful Golion Gerwagg.**

Scratching her head, Talula fumbled in her cloak. *You're a puppet? The most powerful mystic, and you're a puppet? And you need to be paid?*

As the single coin dropped into the slot, the puppet came to life, moving with the wires pulling him from side to side. As he spoke in a pre-recorded robotic voice, a wire pulled his wooden mouth up and down. "Ask Golion Gerwagg, the all-powerful, your question." He flopped forward.

"Urm," Talula said, checking over her shoulders to make sure it wasn't a joke. "I want to know how to kill the Garn?"

The wooden puppet jiggled from side to side as the base of the wooden case clanked and hissed. A flap in the middle of his hands opened, and a glowing glass sphere rose from below and locked in place.

"Golion Gerwagg will now consult the *Sight of Passing.*"

Sight of Passing Talula thought. *That's what the Garn wants. But it's just a glass ball.*

The wooden puppet rumbled and shuffled about as a light bulb pinged on above his head. "The answer to the question can be found below." A small white card was pushed out of a slot.

Checking over her shoulders again, Talula reached into the slot and pulled out a business card. Flipping it over it, she found one word on the back.

"Of course," she said aloud. "How did I miss that!"

Golion Gerwagg moved again, this time more like a human, and his voice became deep and firm. "I have been here since the beginning of time and have seen it all. You now have a choice, Talula Airheart. It is not too late for you. Think carefully about what you do next. The world is finely balanced. One decision will take you on a path to virtue, another will ultimately bring about your demise."

The world stood still for a few seconds … then, her eyes glowing red, Talula clenched her fist and punched through the glass case, grabbing the *Sight of Passing*. "I'm afraid I must follow the path of power to free my friends." She could feel his tiny wooden hands clutch her wrist, but with a flick of her fingers, the inside of the case erupted in a blaze of green flames.

As Talula walked away, the smoky air filled with the sound of glass cracking from the heat. She jumped when out of nowhere a spectre burst out from within the flames. The phantom slowly transformed from the little wooden puppet into a human boy before growing older and older into a man. The male, glowing so bright Talula had to shield her eyes, spoke in a voice which echoed through to her very bones.

"Talula Airheart, your destiny was never finalised until now! You had a choice. The end of your life was clouded, especially so after you met the Threepwood boy. You could have done the right thing, but you sealed your fate by taking one of my many lives. You will die holding the *Divider of Fabric and Space* but not in a way you can imagine. You will be seeing more of me, Talula. Very, very soon." With that, the spectre of Golion Gerwagg vanished.

CHAPTER 34

A glance in the heart of time....

Forcing her way through the rough fibres of the tapestry, Talula walked cautiously down the steps. As she pushed through and landed in the square courtyard, she could feel the glass ball, the *Sight of Passing*, in the left pocket of her robes, weighing her down. She'd felt queasy from the moment she touched it, but she suddenly felt lightheaded and her muscles weak. Barely able to stand, she staggered into the wall, using it for support. Her head felt foggy as large silver circles formed before her eyes.

Talula blinked, suddenly finding herself on a glowing silver path in a forest, the intense bright light burning her retinas. Time slowed, the air growing thick and hard to move through. Her thigh grew warm as the *Light of Passing* pulsated in her pocket. She took it out, holding it out in front of her.

She took a step. A baby cried behind her. With another step, a soft familiar voice filled the air.

"I am sorry, Talula, I just can't live like this anymore. I have to leave."

"Mum?" she whispered.

"I'll come back for you, my darling girl. I'll come back. I promise. I'm so sorry." Talula felt a warm kiss on her forehead.

She took another step, and a harsher voice said, "Glen, you're drunk. Why don't you do this another day? I'll make an appointment for you."

"Look, Vicar, I'm here and I'm doing this now! I'm registering the birth as Talula. I'll fill the form in, and I'll be gone. Now, are you going to show me where to write it?"

Heaving boots stomped away as a baby cried in his arms.

Talula watched another ripple in time. Her father, Glen Airheart, charging out of the church, holding her as a baby. Talula could never remember her mother, but she recalled her voice, her touch.

"Sister," the Vicar's voice said solemnly in her memory, followed by the unmistakable rustle of paper. "That poor girl. He's not even spelt her name right. Talula, instead of Tallulah."

The harsher voice rang through her ears, "Lula! Stop messing about. This is important. Climb through that window. There, you see it. Climb through, drop down and open this door. Don't fall or I'll leave you here. Do you understand?"

As Talula's vision continued, other voices danced around her mind: old school teachers, Lyreco in the forest, Jimmy's first words to her.

She stopped in front of a fork in the road.

To the left was Jimmy. The world around him was obliterated, but they had succeeded, and they could be together. The ashes of the world clouded the other images. To the right was a path less travelled. Talula saw the tear in the fabric of space and time, the glowing vortex showing her an alternative ending. A choice she would need to make. The ending Golion Gerwagg had spoken of.

The blood drained from her face as she came out of the vision. The queasiness grew worse, her head spinning. She pushed away from the wall, stumbling down the hall towards the cell door as she tried to shake off the cobwebs from her mind.

Grinning back from the other side, the Garn reached through the bars. "Did you get it? Did you get the *Sight of Passing*? Don't forget we had a deal."

Still struggling to come to terms with the vision, Talula reached into her pocket and took out the sphere. It clanked against the bars as she pushed it forward. The Garn snatched it from her grasp. The instant it left her hand, the ring with the bobbing arrow in the middle faded. She rubbed her hand on her robe and the mark smudged, like pen ink. Licking the tops of her fingers, Talula scrubbed her hand, erasing the mark.

The Garn laughed. "You've seen it, haven't you? You've seen how it ends?" The creature's eyes glowed white, and the glass ball hummed in her grasp. "You have no idea what this is, yet it revealed to you a glimpse of what will be. Yes, I can see it. You had two choices, one to salvation, and the other will lead to your death. Hope for you was lost when you killed Golion Gerwagg."

The Garn's head moved in slow, methodical movements, as though she was looking into the very heart of time. "I can see everything, Talula, everything! And it doesn't end well for you or your friends. I can also see what you have in your pocket, but it's too late. In a moment, I will be gone, but we shall meet again, yes, a few years from now. When you see me once more, know the end will be near. But for now…" The creature's voice echoed, becoming distant. "…you should be more concerned about your friends. If you leave now, you may just make it."

Talula dived forward, grabbing the bars as she scrabbled in her pockets, but in a blaze of intense light, the creature disappeared. The glass ball bounced twice on the concrete floor, but before Talula could move, it imploded and vanished.

Talula paused, thinking back to why she had come to the dungeons in the first place. Suddenly, the vile image of Daisy Del a Terre flooded her mind, and her stomach twisted with fear. "Jimmy!" she shouted, panicked, and charged back down the hallway.

CHAPTER 35

The weakness exposed….

Hearing the raised voices, Talula ran towards Daisy's room. The wooden door exploded outward just before she reached it, and Jimmy crashed to the floor, landing on his back. He jumped up, his eyes burning red with fury as he ignited his hands in a blaze of green electricity.

Talula held a glimmer of hope that he was battling Daisy, but as she peered around the corner, her worst fears became reality. Jimmy's sword slashed a scorch mark across Harry's chest. Harry's robe split open as he dropped to one knee. Before Jimmy had time to follow through, Percy kicked him hard to the ribs, then unleashed a jet of fire, launching Jimmy through the air where he crashed hard into the wall above the fireplace. Jimmy landed face-first on the floor where a heavy picture frame slammed down onto his back. He tried to push himself up with the last of his strength but collapsed back onto the floor.

Percy staggered towards Jimmy, his legs dripping blood. Jimmy sat up, holding his ribs with one hand while thrusting a sharp piece of wood out in front of him with the other.

Wearing her frilly white summer dress, Daisy stood watching, her hair perfect, as if she'd just stepped out of a salon. "Wait!" she shouted, "it seems we have a guest, boys. Show our new guest what tricks you have learnt."

Like zombies, Percy turned to face Talula as Jimmy and Harry pulled themselves to their feet. In unison, they stomped forward.

Her hands dripping fire, Talula backed out of the doorway, losing her footing on the shards of wood from the demolished door. She stared into Jimmy's glowing red eyes and tried to clear her mind. In the background, Daisy clapped joyfully. Talula gave a slight shake of her head and lowered her hands, her muscles tightening when Jimmy took a firm hold of her right arm. Harry grabbed the left, and they escorted her back into the room and pinned her against the wall. By the time Talula looked up, Daisy's beauty had drained away, leaving behind a foul, slimy Garn, trails of sticky goop in her wake.

"You have done well, my pets," the Garn said to the three boys, who dripped blood from their many cuts and abrasions, barely able to stand. The Garn walked to the side of Talula's face and whispered, "In a moment, I will get them to kill you, then I will watch them fight each other to the death. All in my honour. Afterwards, I'll finally be able to leave this wretched skin." A black, slug-like tongue slipped out of her mouth and licked Talula's cheek before sliding into her ear. Turning, the creature giggled and walked to the centre of the room, where she rummaged in her cloak, pulling out a small compact mirror.

With her attention drawn away, Talula turned to Jimmy. "Jimmy, are you in there? Help me. She's going to kill us all. Help me!"

When Jimmy didn't react, she kicked him hard in the shin with her free foot. "Jimmy! Help me."

His red eyes cracked and flickered like a television on a stormy day. Shaking his head, they turned bright red once more, his grip on her arm tightening.

"My Master, I have them," the Garn said. "The girl is trapped, pinned to the wall. On my command, her beloved friends will kill her without a second thought. The other three are barely standing. They are my puppets. They will all be dead very soon."

The face staring back at her creaked as the ends of his lips turned up in his leathery skin. "Good. Make it quick. I don't want any mistakes. Once you are finished, return to me and you will be rewarded handsomely by my backer."

Clicking the mirror shut, the Garn turned and smiled at Talula. She walked over in a trail of slime and ran her finger down Talula's face. "How to kill you, how to kill you, I wonder. Percy," she shouted. "Pick up the axe!"

As the Garn turned away, Talula felt Jimmy's grip loosen ever so slightly. She looked up into his eyes, finding them brown and full of life instead of red. When he offered her a slight nod, Talula guided her hand into her pocket. Taking a big handful of salt, she waited for the Garn to turn back towards her, then pulled away from Jimmy's grip and threw it into her face.

The silent pause felt as though it lasted an eternity. Talula's heart almost stopped beating. But when the Garn's body finally registered what had happened, the room was suddenly filled with horrific, high-pitched screams. "What have you done? What have you done to me!?" Screaming in agony, she pulled her hands from her face. Her skin bubbled and popped, spurting yellow liquid across the floor. Dropping to her knees, the Garn again clutched her face, "Help me! Help me!" she pleaded, thrashing on the floor, yellow ooze and sizzling steam seeping through her fingers. With a final groan, she slumped down, followed by a loud crunch reverberating through the room.

"The mirror, the mirror," Talula shouted as she skidded forward, plunging her hands into the thick, sticky gunk, trying to feel for the mirror in the creature's pocket. In unison behind her, the boys gasped and collapsed to the floor, wincing in pain as they clutched their many wounds.

Talula fumbled through the sludge for the rounded plastic surface. Stretching as far as she could, her scrunched face turned away from the foul smell, she finally pinched the mirror in her fingers and thrust herself backwards. Gagging, she tried to hold back the vomit as she wiped the case on her cloak and clicked it open. Two long cracks streaked through the centre of the glass as it wobbled and came to life. The cracks made it impossible to see anything but black images, but there was sound.

"You have done well, Imjimn-Ra," a distorted voice said in the distance to one of the images.

"Yes," another, more familiar voice groaned. "Once they are dead, the next part of our plan can take place. We will force the elders from their tower. One by one, they will be destroyed."

The first voice spoke again, "Now, Imjimn-Ra, you must sever the link between the elders and the Gatekeeper. Soon we shall be rulers of this world, as we were promised."

One of the pieces of glass wriggled free from the plastic. As it did, the imaged turned to glass once more and all that remained was Talula staring at her own exhausted, battered face.

What do they mean by 'force the elders from their tower?' She turned and ran to her friends.

Behind the group, the Garn's shrivelled body continued to smoulder, the soggy patch below her body slowly widening. As the puddle expanded, it formed into a tiny round head, then dragged whatever it could of itself towards a vent on the floor.

As Talula turned back to make sure the creature was dead, she found the expanding puddle had vanished.

CHAPTER 36

The siege of the Unearthly Prison....

Jimmy's awoke days later in a medical room being poked and prodded by LaForte, the tips of her giant ogre fingers slimy and sticky. Half unconscious, he vaguely remembered hoping it wasn't snot. Every one of Jimmy's muscles ached as he lay there staring at the ceiling of his room, writhing in agony at even the slightest movement. His whole body felt as though it had gone through the spin cycle on the washing machine.

He tried his hardest to think back to what had happened. What would make him fight the others and try to hurt Talula? All that pushed through the fog in his mind was that fragrance. The sweet, yet oaky smell that wrapped his body in warm cotton wool and released him into the deepest, most refreshing dreams he'd ever had. As his eyes became heavy, the euphoric feeling flooded back. He drifted in a dreamlike state, a faint smile pulling up his lips. The Garn may have been dead but the effects of her powers still lingered deep in his mind. His arm started to reach out in front of him to touch the mirage when three heavy thumps hit his door, snapping him awake.

"Jimmy!" Majordomo shouted. "Jimmy, hurry, we need you … the council needs you now! Come quickly."

Jimmy sprang from the bed without thinking, and a thousand hot needles stabbed into his muscles. Hopping to the door, he opened it and saw his three weary companions covered head to toe in scars and bruises. "Master Jimmy,"

Majordomo said, "you have been summoned to the Council of Elders. Please ready yourself. We must leave in haste."

Jimmy could see the worry on Majordomo's face, but his three companions would only stare at the floor.

Emptying his mind, he thought only of the elders as he sunk into the floor. Fresh crisp air blew into his face as he stepped over the threshold into the Vantage Room. It took a moment for his eyes to adjust to the bright white light. Jimmy thought back to the many times he had been summoned to the elders since returning to Sepura Castle after finding the *Elixir of Light*, but something felt different this time. Something was wrong.

The normally tranquil, sky-blue flooring with the odd fluffy cloud was replaced by an angry-looking grey colour that screamed with worry. Black clouds streaked in regimented lines through the centre of the room.

"Oler, what do you mean the connection has been severed?!" he heard Trident roar from the twelve o'clock position at the head of the circle of chairs.

Next to Trident, the projected image of the old man's head started to groan, and though his mouth was barely visible through his beard, he replied, "Master, it's gone. We have lost the connection. We can no longer summon the Gatekeeper."

A chorus of groans and grumbles came from the other eight people sitting in chairs facing Trident. They looked to him for leadership and support. Standing directly behind Trident's white, egg-shaped seat was Professor Will Potts. His eyes remained shut, his arms folded tightly across his chest.

Lord Trident glanced towards the empty seat next to Oler Roindex, the seat once occupied by Huic Ostiarius. Wrapped in cobwebs, it was unlike the others. No menacing, projected face stared back at Jimmy. "Then it is true," Trident said, his voice quieter, as though deep in thought. Looking up, Trident noticed his four new guests. Spluttering, he adjusted what remained of his human body behind the image and cleared his throat.

The four companions pushed through the aggressive black clouds and climbed the three white steps. Walking into the centre of the open circle, they each knelt and remained focused only on the shiny white floor.

"Argh, my children, you have arrived at a grave time." Lord Trident paused when the ruby crystal Professor Potts held suddenly glowed with intensity. His eyes opened wide, and he walked like a robot to Jimmy Threepwood and handed him the crystal ball. Turning slowly, he walked off again without saying a word, taking his place behind Trident.

Jimmy angled the crystal to the light and read aloud the words that appeared in rainbow colours within the stone. "We, the Diamond Giants of Andorrump, have laid siege to the Unearthly Prison, and the Gatekeeper is our prisoner. Our demands are simple. We require the Council of Elders to leave the sanctity of the Forgotten Garden and re-enter their human forms. Once they are again flesh and blood, they will enter the Unearthly Prison to become our prisoners. As a token of good faith, we will allow two days for a decision. If the Council of Elders do not arrive, every living soul trapped within the prison will be released."

"But it's a trap!" Lorratt Del-Vargo shouted, trying to squeeze his head tightly into the projection. "We left our human form centuries ago. I don't even know if mine still works."

"If we don't," Aralynn said sternly, "and the souls are released, the Diamond Giants could control them, forge them into an unstoppable army."

Panic took hold as the eight council members all started shouting over the top of one another.

Ignoring the rumblings going on around them, Jimmy thought back to the words on the crystal, '*The Gatekeeper is our prisoner.*' The edges of his lips turned up. *Good!* His eyes started to glow. *At last, you are getting what you deserve. Hopefully, the elders will fail, and you get what's coming to you.*

"Silence!" Lord Trident shouted. They all stopped and pushed back further into their holograms. "You remember what Huic Ostiarius did! You know he tried to steal the Rose Pen. You saw what he did to Majordomo … and you know of his punishment." He focused on the bottom of his chair. "The entrance to the Unearthly Prison has been sealed for centuries. The only way in or out was through the mirror. It seems that has either been destroyed or our signal somehow blocked. There is no way to enter even if we wanted too."

The room grew silent. Rosaland Fellaini mumbled something, then stopped.

"Rosaland?" Lord Trident said with authority.

"Well, I understood there was a second mirror, an exact copy made by the Altered Wizards, to help keep a watchful eye on the world."

Trident groaned, breathing past the bristles in his moustache. Giving Rosaland an ugly stare, he spoke again, "Then it is decided. You four…" He nodded in the direction of Jimmy. "…will seek out the Altered Wizards. I am sure if they don't wish to help you, you will figure out a way to make them understand the urgency of the situation. You will enter the Unearthly Prison and free the Gatekeeper, help him take back control. Do you understand?"

It took a long time for the words to sink into Jimmy's mind. His face and neck grew hot at the surge of anger boiling in his blood. His breathing became short and sharp, his hands shaking.

"No!" Jimmy shouted defiantly as he broke formation. "No! I will not help that ... that monster. Let the giants rid the world of him. I was told you would help me! Our combined strength would destroy the Gatekeeper. But you never had any intention of helping me, did you? Did you!?"

The elders gasped and glanced at Trident.

Trident diverted his gaze from Rosaland. "You will do you as you are told, Jimmy Threepwood!" Professor Potts came to life behind him but was stopped in mid-step. "I am your master."

The floor behind Jimmy became as black as night. The shiny surface of the platform hardened like cement around Jimmy's feet. Ice crawled over his legs, locking them in place. The liquid blue ice entered his body and slithered along his main veins and arteries, through his chest and into his face. Jimmy screamed, trying desperately to move, but he was trapped. The ice-cold liquid burnt through his blood.

"You may be powerful, Jimmy Threepwood, but you are still no match for me."

Jimmy winced, in agony, the fiery colour draining from his face and eyes.

Talula started to lunge forward to help, but Percy grabbed her sleeve. "No, leave it. He has to learn. They won't hurt him. They need him."

Clenching his teeth, Jimmy's whole body dropped to the floor when Trident released his grip.

"Be very wary, my children," Trident said in a quiet tone filled with authority and warning. "If you dare challenge me, you will never win, and I can assure you the battle will be very painful. Now go, get out of my sight! Find the Altered Wizards and free the Gatekeeper."

The moment he stopped speaking, Talula and Percy grabbed Jimmy and helped carry him back down the steps. As they walked, birds flitted around them, and the floor under their feet once again turned sky-blue.

As Percy dragged Jimmy over the threshold, Talula gave one final glance over her shoulder. *Don't worry, Lord Trident, your time is coming to an end. You will all be destroyed, and I'll make sure this world is put right in our image, just like you promised so many times before.*

CHAPTER 37

Don't be too hasty....

Snorting steam, the four black horses galloped through the air on an invisible road, flying with their bat-like wings. Wild animals charged through the forest below, trying to escape the shadows cast by the enormous, threatening beasts.

"There!" Harry yelled, pointing into the distance. The others couldn't hear over the howling winds and their flapping hoods, but they looked towards where he pointed.

Far in the distance, a jagged black mountain top came into view, clouds hiding its massive base. Strong winds and streaks of lightning circled it counter clockwise.

Undeterred by the storm, the four riders thundered forward, their hair standing on end as their horses pushed through the highly charged atmosphere. Circling the mountain, they look for a safe place to settle on the jagged surface. Harry pointed to a small patch of flat ground at the base. With a nod of agreement from Talula, they circled once more and swooped down, coming to a halt on the ground, where they dismounted.

A tube-shaped barrier of energy fizzed and crackled around them, shooting up into the sky as far as their eye could see. Directly above them, most of the mountain was shrouded by thick clouds.

"Look," Harry said. "Steps." He pointed to a staircase carved into the rock face leading high into the distance. "This way," he shouted, grabbing Percy by the arm. "Come on." They ran off.

"I think we should wait, have a look around first!" Talula shouted after them, but Harry and Percy were already halfway up the first set of steps.

As they disappeared around the back of the mountain, Talula noticed a small wooden sign poking out from the ground in front of some dry shrubs and bushes. As she approached, the letters gradually came into focus.

Everlasting Highway: Please watch your body

*

"We've been walking for hours," Percy said, slowly lumbering up the steps one by one.

"Come on, stop moaning," Harry shouted back. He was two steps ahead, visible beads of sweat resting on his brow. "It can't be far now. We must be nearing the summit."

Percy peered over the edge into the nothingness. Below them, as far as the eye could see, clouds of static-charged electricity spit and crackled through the air. "I can't see Talula or Jimmy."

"I told you," Harry said, craning his neck, "it's got to be just ahead." Harry struggled to put on a brave face, his calves killing him. They kept seizing up, making every step agony. As he plodded to the next corner, he was sure it had to be the top. His spirit plummeted when he turned the corner and found yet more steps leading to the heavens. Harry looked up.

"We're barely halfway there." Defeated, he went to sit on the floor. "I give up."

With a clunk and a clank, the steps flattened into a smooth, shiny surface, and like a helter-skelter, they slid around and around, gaining momentum the whole time. When they reached the bottom, the slide angled slightly upward. The pair hit the ramp at great speed, their bodies soaring through the air to land with a crash next to where Talula and Jimmy sat patiently waiting.

With multi-coloured stars glowing before his eyes, Harry could just about hear Talula's tinny voice. "Where have you been? We've been worried sick."

Harry looked over at her, his vision blurred, and rubbed his head to try to push down the protruding lump, "Calm down, Talula, we've only been gone a few hours."

"A few hours!" Talula snapped. "A few hours? More like a few days! You ran off two days ago. We've been sat here like fools ever since. Don't you ever think about what you're doing?"

Talula's rant was halted by the clanking of the mountain as it released compressed gas through tiny vents in the side. With a loud crunch, the tiny slats in the slide popped forward, returning them to solid stone steps.

Pushing himself up, Percy stretched and dusted off his robes. "I don't think that's the way in."

Talula glared as she replied sharply, "No, but you ran off before we had a chance to look."

"We think we've found something," Jimmy said, trying to cut through the tension.

Jimmy and Talula walked to the wooden sign poking up from the mound of earth, followed by Harry and Percy. Kicking aside some dust, he exposed a black wire running from the back of the wooden sign under the shrubs to a waist-high metal lever with a bicycle safely break at the top. Jimmy squeezed the break and pulled it to the right, but it only moved a few inches, locked in place by rust.

Harry stepped to the side of Jimmy and pushed, while Percy grabbed the other side and pulled. The lever gradually moved but was also bending under the pressure. With one final pull, the lever gave way and clicked into position.

From the base of the mountain came an angry scream and a hollow roar. More steam pumped out of the vents. A loud squeaking noise, that sounded like unoiled cogs scraping against one another, filled the air as the steps moved forward a metre, then jerked to a stop. With a loud bang, as though the coils had managed to break free, the steps rotated forward and upward like an escalator in a supermarket. The unmistakable smell of sulphur and burning rust filled the air.

"That's the way in," Talula said as she walked off.

As soon as her back was turned, Harry pulled a mimicking face and mumbled quietly to Percy, "Now that's the way in, la de da."

Jimmy kicked the bottom stone step as it rolled past him. Holding onto the sides, timing it just right, he jumped onto the bottom step, then looked back to make sure everyone else had got on. As all four of them stood in a line on the stone escalator, they drifted through the clouds. The dry static charge wreaked havoc with Talula's hair, causing it to puff out at the ends. She repeatedly flattened them against her face.

As the escalator reached the midpoint of the mountain, a purple door opened in front of them. They passed through it into the darkness. Though they were no longer climbing, the escalator continued to shuffle through the dark. Flashing warning lights poked out of the ground on metal stalks, illuminating the stone walls once every two seconds. A disembodied voice broke the silence, shouting repeatedly, "Warning, warning, you are reaching the end of the Everlasting Highway. Pease watch your body as you disembark. Take your arms and legs with you."

Watch your body? Jimmy thought as he stepped on to the metal grid. *Take your arms and legs with you?*

The others followed quickly. As they stood in a line, six poisonous darts hissed out of either side of the walls, flying directly at them.

CHAPTER 38

The passageway to the Unearthly Prison....

Talula held her arms out at waist height, her eyes igniting into a blaze of fire. The room froze, leaving the tiny silver darts suspended in mid-air about half an inch from each of their necks. Anger surged when she glanced over at Jimmy, seeing the needle touching his cheek, a tiny trickle of blood dribbling down his face. She refocused back on the darts, and one by one, destroyed the needles molecule by molecule until there was nothing left.

Snarling, Talula thrust her hands forward. Two large cracks ripped through the centre of the walls on either side of where they stood. As time caught up, the walls separated and smashed onto the floor, filling the room with dust and rubble. Twenty or thirty more darts hissed from their capsules and ricochet around the chamber. One came close enough that Percy heard it whistle past his ear.

As the darts stopped firing, the ground began to rumble beneath Jimmy's feet. The four companions stared at each other, then ducked just as a hundred black bats flashed over their heads. They flickered around them as they searched for openings in the mountain walls, then disappeared out into the human realm.

"Go on then," Talula snapped at Harry. She nodded towards doors three times their height being illuminated by the flashing amber lights. "You're normally first."

Harry nodded, a frown on his face as he glanced towards her hands, as though worried about what she might do next.

Jimmy didn't wait for Harry. He approached the doors first, turning the black ring handles. The giant doors creaked open. Only a faint flicker of light could be seen in the back of the dark room. The other three followed him as he stepped over the threshold, twitching as the door slammed shut behind them. They could hear something scuttling across the floor ahead.

Stepping back, Jimmy tried to prepare himself for whatever might attack.

"Show yourself," Percy shouted.

Talula's hands burst into green flames as she took a step forward. As the shadows came alive, a screaming face appeared from the darkness and shoved her so hard that she fell backwards, crashing into the others.

The creature screamed at them as it stomped forward, sparks fizzling from the end of its long fingernails. The extra bit of light brought its disfigured face into view as it yelled, "Get out of here! What do you want? How dare you enter my sanctuary. I will rip you to pieces." It slashed forward, casting singe marks across the door.

Jimmy unleashed a small bolt of electricity into the creature's chest. As it staggered back, an electric javelin formed in Jimmy's hand, humming to life between his fingers. He lowered the power in the weapon, aware they needed to question the creature. He threw the bolt into its shoulder, and it yelped in pain as the electrical charge ripped through its nervous system. Its legs turned to jelly, and it dropped to its knees.

"I will get you!" the creature groaned. It twisted its body around, exposing a second face, exactly the same as the first, except for the expression of horror. "Please don't hurt me," the second face said. "Please, please don't hurt us."

The first face winced in pain, but shouted, "Shut up, you fool! I will kill them. Turn back around! Turn back around."

The eyes on the second face turned in every direction, as though searching for an escape. It kept turning its waist, but the other half of its body, still trembling with electricity, wouldn't respond. In desperation, it twisted its body the other way, and a third face and new pair of legs came into view.

Though just as hideous as the other two, this face was calm and reserved. "Please, Children of Tyranacus, don't hurt us. We had to make sure it was you."

"Kill them," the first voice screamed once again.

"Shh ... please excuse us." Clicking his three-fingered hands together, fires ignited in every corner.

Harry's mouth dropped open in awe as he took in the creature in front of him. He couldn't help but stare at the three human bodies fused together to make one person ... one thing.

"We are the Altered Wizards." It took a few steps back, dragging the third member, who was still spitting and hissing in anger.

"Take what you want. Take it all and just go," said the second head, who was still cringing. It faced away from them, desperately trying to avoid eye contact.

"Ignore my brothers. It is difficult for us. We haven't had any visitors for a long time."

The aggressive creature started to stir, groaning.

Twisting his body, the sensible creature turned and started fumbling on a table behind it. The twisting motion turned the second creature to face the group. Squeezing its eyes shut, it refused to try to talk to them.

Twisting back around, the sensible head held a long hollow tube in its grasp. The thin wooden tube had a series of tiny holes running throughout it. Reaching back, the scared body also grabbed a tube. The aggressive body muttered under its breath but finally took its tube when repeatedly nudged.

Holding the tubes out in front of them, the tips touched, creating a triangle. With a slight change in the room's air pressure, all the creature's eyes began to glow in unison.

"We are the Altered Wizards," said the creatures in a different voice, a single, distant voice. "We have been expecting you." It diverted its eyes to a singed piece of paper on the floor. "You seek entry to the Unearthly Prison. You seek to free the Gatekeeper of life and death?" A large piece of furniture rolled across the floor on wheels into the centre of the room. The velvet cover slipped off, exposing a grand mirror inside a glowing frame of gold. The mirror's surface wobbled and turned black.

As the glass cleared, a cloaked figure chained to a wall came into view. Patrolling the room were two enormous guards that appeared to be made from solid diamond. They each had one large eye in the middle of their faces, which scrutinised the Gatekeeper's every movement.

The image faded to black.

"This is the last mirror, the final point of entry into the Unearthly Prison. But heed my warning ... if you go through, there is no way back."

The companions stared at one another, each wondering what would happen if they returned to Sepura Castle without freeing the Gatekeeper. They would have to take their chances.

"So be it," said the Wizards.

The mirror turned black and spun rapidly on its axis. It stopped after the fifth spin and split in half, creating a glowing, humming, amethyst door. Through the swoosh of sucking air, the children heard the Wizards say, "The prophecy will die with them."

Talula, Jimmy and Harry immediately stepped through the door into the unknown. Percy stopped and turned back, shouting to be heard over the noise, "What happened to you? Did a spell go wrong?"

The Altered Wizards smiled. "We were once three powerful sorcerers, young Percy, tasked with balancing the Earth, but..." It looked down at its disfigured, melted body, "...this is what happens when you don't do as Lord Trident commands."

CHAPTER 39

The watch is mightier than any sword....

The doorway crumpled after Percy was pulled into the vortex of the mirror. It imploded in a haze of crackles and sparks behind him. He could feel the slight, but noticeable change in the atmosphere, the thinner air more difficult to breathe. He became lightheaded, his eyelids heavy.

Someone grabbed his arm. He opened his eyes to see Talula and the others staring at him. He sat up and studied his surroundings, finding the blackness littered with millions of round, studded stars. Warning alarms boomed as thousands of metal cell doors chattered open, then slammed shut a few seconds later. After a few moments, screams of terror filled the air.

In front of them, thousands upon thousands of humans formed single lines leading to waist-high metal conveyer belts. At the front of each machine, directed by at least two towering black shadows, the prisoners reluctantly emptied their pockets, then removed jackets and shoes before being shoved through a seven-foot rectangular scanner. If the scanner activated, the guards would manhandle the culprit and search them thoroughly. Once the checks were completed, a glowing white disk appeared on the floor beneath their feet, and they were transported to one of the stars, or as the children now realized, cells.

Firm hands pushed Percy forward into the others. When he turned to face it, two dripping black fangs snarled back at him. Percy's hands sparked to life, but then he felt a tap on his shoulder. Turning around, he found thousands of black flickering souls surging towards them like a plague of locusts.

"Percy, leave it," Talula said from behind him.

Percy stared into the hollow, lifeless eyes of the fanged creature, then glanced at the approaching army. Thinking better of it, he extinguished the spark in his hands.

The creature shoved Percy again and raised a sharp claw to point towards an empty conveyer belt. Percy struggled to swallow down his fury, knowing this wasn't the right time to fight. The conveyer belt came to life as he shuffled forward, carrying with it a grey plastic tray. It stopped in front of Jimmy, and a black flickering creature stepped into view and pointed to a sign nailed to the wall.

"No mortal items are allowed in the Unearthly Prison. Please remove all watches, weapons and rings," Jimmy read aloud. Patting down his pockets, he removed his cloak and shoes, placing them in the tray. Stepping forward, he held his breath as he watched the intimidating red and green lights on the imposing machine. A red warning light screamed in his ear, and he was grabbed by several pairs of strong hands and vigorously searched. Reaching into his left pocket, the shadow pulled out a shiny pocket watch suspended on a thin metal chain.

The watch, Jimmy thought as he patted the left side of his chest—where it was normally stored in his robes. He looked over to where his robe had just reappeared through the other end of the conveyer belt. *How did it get in my trouser pocket?* The engraved letters on the back glowed, spelling DOLT.

The flickering black creature growled, slamming the watch down hard on a wooden table in front of the conveyer belt.

Jimmy stood at the end of the system and waited for the others to join him. The alarm was also raised for Percy. Jimmy watched as they seized an item from him.

All four stood in a line as white disks appeared one by one beneath their feet. Jimmy felt someone fumbling for his fingers. When he looked up, he found Talula smiling back at him.

"Where do you think we're going, Jimmy?" she whispered. "A cell? How are we going to get—?"

Talula's question was cut off by a sinister, booming voice reverberating around the empty space. "No, Talula, you will not be joining these pathetic humans as they await entrance to their eternal prisons. You, Talula, have arrived here a little earlier than expected. Nevertheless, you are here and will be granted access as a mortal with the other three. You are here to rescue the Gatekeeper, but be warned, this is a one-way journey. There is no way out. We have taken complete control of this realm. Once you are dead, we plan to release the flickering souls to ravage the mortal world."

The disks below their feet faded, and a fist-sized purple hole appeared, tearing a hole through the fabric of space.

"This will be a deadly journey for all four of you, and to make sure you have at least some chance, I will allow you to bring one weapon, or an item of your choice. Choose wisely," said the unknown voice before it began to roar with laughter. "It won't do you much good against the undisputable power of the Diamond Giants."

The wooden table vibrated and shook as an assortment of weapons and the group's personal items reappeared. Harry broke formation and grabbed a long-bladed sword, slicing it through the air. Concentrating, he channelled his power into the weapon, and it burst into flames.

Talula watched what Harry had done and reached for a shield.

Jimmy studied the shinning arsenal carefully, noticing his pocket watch. As he stroked the shiny metal, he felt it hum under his touch. Running his fingers across the engraving, he suddenly heard the voice of Mr Gibbs in his ear, the Watchmaker.

"The time will come soon when you will need this watch. Remember, the watch is mightier than any sword."

Jimmy paused for only a moment, then picked up the watch and shoved it into his pocket.

Percy had picked up an axe and was judging its weight when Jimmy caught the twinkle of light coming from a gold ring. A smile spread across his face as he nudged Percy with his elbow. "The *Ring of Vision*." He pointed towards it.

Percy dropped the axe and picked up the ring between his fingers. As he rolled it back and forth, he felt it. For the first time since he had won the ring all those years ago, it showed a hint of power. As he slid it onto his right index finger, Percy's eyes glazed over, turning pure black.

He slowly opened his eyes, speaking in a distant voice, "I have seen it, Jimmy. I have seen how we can escape this realm."

CHAPTER 40

The cloaked prisoner….

The intense heat hit them like a brick wall when they stepped through the fabric of space. A thin stone path ran through the centre of smoking lava, which smashed violently against the corroded catacomb walls. Flakes of brittle grey ash littered the air, and distant screams bounced off the cavern walls.

The groans became louder as hundreds of black, flickering souls surfaced from below the fire. Pushing through the flames, the souls waded towards the path, steam rising from their scorched skin. Reaching the path, they appeared blocked by an invisible barrier. All the lunging forward and thrashing of their claws sent waves of bubbling lava onto the path which sizzled then quickly evaporated.

Talula was the first to move forward, pointing out a grand stone door at the far end of the path. Within two steps, the group could feel the rubber on the bottom of their shoes melting into the ground, mixing together with the awful foul smell of burnt bacon and melted plastic. Afraid their shoes might burn off, and with hundreds of squirming black claws snapping at their ankles, they picked up their pace.

Jimmy tried to dance on the path around the claws, but they took hold of the hem of his trousers, stopping him in his tracks. As he jerked free, he tried to ignore the intense heat burning his feet, only to face one groaning soul who'd managed to crawl its way up on the path. The soul hissed as the inky blackness covering its mouth started to melt away.

"You have been wrong all this time, Jimmy Threepwood," it said in a weak, cracked voice. "He is not dead. He was killed when it wasn't his time. He is not dead, but he is lost in the void. You can still save him. Never give up, Jimmy Threepwood. He can be saavedd."

As soon as the creature spoke its final word, the blackness crawled back over its face and it sank into the depths of the lava.

Jimmy remained silent, thinking back over every syllable the creature had uttered, his emotions burning like the fire through his socks. Jumping from foot to foot, he spotted the others at the far end of the path, pushing and prodding at the thick stone door. He ran to catch up, confused about what soul the creature might have spoken of.

The instant Jimmy's feet touched the platform, the door grumbled and groaned. As stone grated against stone, the door slowly crawled open. Staring back at them from the widening gap was an enormous eye. The blue glass eye stared out, while hands the size of cars were planted on each side of the floor. The ground started to shake as the eyeball disappeared, and the colossal body clambered to its feet. Staring down at them through the gap, the juggernaut flashed a rainbow of colours in every direction, the light shimmering off millions of tiny sparkling diamonds.

Sensing danger, the companions took two steps back, still very aware of the shadowy claws near the floor that were nipping at their ankles. With a crash that sounded like thunder tearing through the sky, an axe almost half the size of the room smashed through the door, sending mountains of rubble and stone tumbling into the lava below.

Trampling through the curtain of steam and fire, the ruby red of the lava reflected off the jewelled body of the colossal giant. The huge, single glass eye resting on its shoulder glared at them as it raised its glass axe high above its head with both hands. It screamed like a barbarian before stomping forward, each step sending fractures throughout the stone path.

With each of its steps, the vibrations rumbled through the ground, causing the companions' bodies to jerk in unison. Percy's mouth went dry as he took in two more giants standing beyond the shattered remnants of the door. The two giants stood closely together, guarding the cloaked Gatekeeper, who dangled by chains. His attention shifted back to the giant with the axe as it smashed another section of the path to pieces.

Pressed back against the wall, Jimmy's palm blazed into life. He created a lightning bolt that crackled in his hand, then launched the charged bolt, sending it sparking through the air, but the Diamond Giant didn't even flinch. The bolt of lightning struck hard against the right shoulder, giving off an empty ping as it dropped and fizzled out, bouncing on the path before it slipped into the flames. A second later, the lava exploded, sending a tidal wave of fire over the path, splashing red-hot magma onto the giant's legs.

As smoke oozed off its body, it stomped forward relentlessly. The companions cowered in its mammoth shadow as the giant planted both feet firmly on the edges of the path, then slowly raised the axe high above his head. They were trapped. There was nothing they could do, no escape.

CHAPTER 41

The indestructible diamond....

Black claws pushed through the river of fire and clamped onto the Diamond Giant's ankle. Tugging and pulling at the juggernaut's foot, the flickering soul screamed, and three more surfaced, digging their nails into the sparkling precious stone.

The glass eye turned its focus from the group to the weak, pathetic insects trying to yank its limb from the path. Lifting its leg in the air, the four souls still clinging to it, the giant slammed it down hard on the path, throwing the souls back into the lava. A hairline fracture in the stone path cracked wider under its foot as the giant returned its attention to the companions.

Jimmy stared at the path, holding his breath as the crack slowly snaked forward. The edge finally gave way under the immense weight of the giant. Thrown off balance, its sparkling leg fell along with the crumbling stone into the fire.

A yellow crackling sword burst to life in his hand as Jimmy charged towards the roaring giant, its leg bursting into flames. With one clean strike, he took out the giant's blue glass eye. As if in slow motion, the eye flew through the air to shatter into a thousand pieces against the stone, covering the path in tiny shards of glass. The axe fell from the giant's grasp as its body went limp.

Seizing their chance, dozens of black claws waded through the lava and dragged the glittering carcass into the flames.

Before they could reach him, Jimmy jumped over the broken section of the path and leapt into air, transforming into a flame-covered phoenix. A trail of fire streaked behind him as Jimmy landed at the feet of the second giant. In one swift motion, he changed back to his human form and struck the creature's arm with his sword. The impact caused the lightning sword to burst into a blaze of white light as it shattered like a piece of cheap glass. With the force of a tank, the Diamond Giant struck Jimmy in the chest with its open palm, throwing him through the air. He slammed into the wall with such force that he visibly shuddered and went limp, sliding down the wall.

Talula unleashed a wave of green fireballs, which staggered the giant. But even so, as they hit its diamond-covered body, they exploded and deflected beams of red-hot light in every direction. One of the wild beams struck Harry in the back, leaving him writhing in agony. The third giant took advantage, striking him hard on the shoulder with the flat side of its axe, and he collapsed to the floor. Another loose beam carved through a stone pillar above Harry. As if in slow motion, the heavy stone blocks tumbled down, pinning him to the floor.

From within the plumes of dust, Percy morphed into a dragon, and now matched the giant in both size and strength. He slashed across the giant's chest, and as it staggered backward, he unleashed a tidal wave of red-hot fire for as long as he could physically hold it. As the steam faded, the giant trampled forward. Standing in front of Percy, it wiped the thick black soot from its chest, revealing an untainted, sparkling diamond. Percy grunted in amazement as the last of his fiery breath puffed out of his nose.

The giant grabbed Percy tightly by the neck and punched him in the jaw with a fist the size of a boulder. Stars spread across his vision as he thrashed and clawed at the juggernaut's body. He could hear the empty metallic sound as his nails chinked off the diamond, the tips of his nails chipping and snapping with every strike. His wings flapped wildly as the giant crushed his windpipe. Percy stared at his reflection in the glass eye, feeling his life force draining away.

Suddenly it hit him; he knew the creature's weakness. With the last of his strength, he flapped his enormous wings as hard as he could, lifting his body off the ground. He hovered just above the giant, getting his rear legs free. Raising one back leg, he struck the tips of his claws as hard as he could into the giant's glass eye.

The Diamond Giant roared, releasing its grip, and as the air flooded back into Percy's lungs, he took flight, his claws still clamped in the creature's eye. As the giant's feet left the floor, it scrambled, managing to grab its axe. The cracking of the glass eye reverberated around the hall as the giant swung at Percy's free claws, slicing through the talons, severing one. As it soared through the air, the talon morphed back into a finger and landed on the floor below. Percy shrieked in pain and released his grip, sending the giant plummeting head-first to the floor. The glass eye exploded on impact.

Percy sent jets of fire and ash into the air as the blood gushed from his severed claw. The colour drained from his scales as he went into shock, shrinking back into his human form while still in the air. Falling, he crashed onto the boulders piled above Harry.

"Percy! Nooo!" Talula screamed as the dust and grime settled over his body.

She could see Harry's lifeless, bruised and battered hand poking out from the rubble, and Percy collapsed on top of the pile. Then there was Jimmy. He coughed weakly in the corner against the wall, struggling to drag himself up.

Talula's eyes widened when she looked back to see the third giant's immense hand gripping, almost crushing, the handle of its glass axe. Her breathing became too quick, too shallow, and her blood felt as though it might start boiling. Clenching her fist, she dropped to her knees and clutched her face with both hands, screaming in pain.

As the giant trampled towards her, it adjusted its grip on the axe, preparing to strike. It growled, starting to raise its axe for the final blow, when the shadow of a bat burst from Talula's back and hovered in the air, staring back with its pig-like face at the giant. The bat released a high-pitched squeal, sending circular sound waves through the air. The waves passed through the giant, and the room fell silent.

Just as it started to pull down sharply with its axe, the Diamond Giant shattered into a million pieces, showering the whole area. Standing up, Talula staggered, losing her balance. Her face felt like it was on fire. She could feel the lines where she had dragged fingernails across it while fighting against the pain.

Crouched over the remains of the shattered giant, Talula didn't know which way to go. She started to move towards Jimmy, then stopped and stepped towards Harry and Percy. Out of the corner of her eye, she saw Jimmy try to pull himself to his feet, and she made up her mind.

Staggering towards Jimmy, she helped him stand. "Jimmy." Sick with worry, she pulled his arm around her shoulder.

"No," Jimmy said weakly, fighting to take a deep breath. "The Gatekeeper, free the Gatekeeper. He's the only one who can get us out of this place. Free him and then get us out."

Pausing, Talula looked at the pile of rubble covering her friends. Though angry, she knew he was right. The Gatekeeper was their only way out of Unearthly Prison.

CHAPTER 42

At last they meet....

As she walked towards the Gatekeeper, Talula noticed the grand mirror sitting eerily in the corner. Shadows flashed over its reflective surface, giving her a feeling of dread, a feeling of being watched. Resting a few steps in front of the mirror was Percy's severed finger. Still attached to it, sparkling amongst the destruction, was his ring, the *Ring of Vision.*

Talula approached the Gatekeeper cautiously. He looked weak and lifeless, hung by his chained arms; the links locked around metal hoops nailed to the wall. She prodded him sharply on the shoulder. When she got no response, she grabbed him with both hands and gave a hard shake. His battered cloak was threadbare, the fabric rotten and covered in tiny slash marks. Her lip curled in disgust as a dirty brown centipede crawled out of one of the holes and slithered over her hand.

Shaking the arthropod loose, she took a harder hold of the Gatekeeper's arm, squeezing. "Gatekeeper, it's me, Talula. We've come to save you."

Snapping his gaze to Talula, his eyes an empty void, lifeless, he laughed, the menacing sound causing her stomach to tighten with dread. "Save me!" He sneered, exposing jagged, chipped teeth. "Save me!"

Talula stepped back as the thick steel chains began to fizzle and dissolve, as though they'd been doused in acid.

He dropped to the floor when the chains snapped. The cloak fell over his bones as he rose slowly, taking one step forward. "The Garn told me you were already dead. I was expecting the elders to enter my prison, not you. But never mind, I will kill you now, then the elders will suffer for what they did to me!"

The Gatekeeper glanced at Jimmy, who was propped up against the wall. He turned back in time to see Talula launch an attack. Holding out his hand, he snatched the fireball from the air and held it tightly in his clenched fist. After blowing on the bony remains of his hand, he opened his fist, releasing a puff of green smoke that floated harmlessly into the air.

Talula turned to run, but the Gatekeeper squeezed his fingers together and thrust his arm forward. Her body locked in place, then was lifted from the floor, suspended, leaving her helpless. Staring into her eyes, the Gatekeeper bore deep into the back of her mind, twisting and distorting her memories, filling her with fear and unimaginable horrors.

As Talula began to tremble and sweat, the Gatekeeper narrowed his eyes to penetrate further, but a sizzling yellow knife sliced through the side of his hood, barely missing his face. Breaking his gaze, he saw Jimmy staring back at him. With a mere flick of his wrist, the Gatekeeper sent Talula flying across the room. She skidded on the stone floor, then crashed into the rubble of the broken wall.

"Jimmy Threepwood," the Gatekeeper snarled. "I'm so glad we are finally being given the chance to talk … alone."

Two swords ignited in Jimmy's hands. The sound snapped around the hall like a whip cracking across the floor.

"I can feel it, Jimmy, the rage swelling beneath your skin. But I can also feel your power! I felt it the day I collected you from your house. Unfortunately, you were restricted by love for your father. The elders sensed it too. They needed to ensure you achieved your potential."

"So, it is you! You are working with the Shadow? It is you trying to kill the elders," snapped Jimmy as the electricity channelled up his arms.

"Did the elders tell you about the Rose Pen, Jimmy?" Anger leaked through Jimmy's pores, but the Gatekeeper could see by his blank expression that they hadn't. "You poor fool. You've been so blinded by anger that you didn't notice what was going on around you. All the Children of Tyranacus before you were offered a bargain. A deal. If they destroyed the earth, they would walk the new world as gods. They would be given the power of the elders … but it was a lie. You've seen what happened to Aurabella and Vesty, cast out alone. But you, your only condition was that you were given the power to kill me, and you dragged your friends in here with you. The elders are using you, Jimmy Threepwood.

"The Rose Pen is the creator of the universe. It drew the trees, the sky, the oceans, but the humans destroyed it all." He clenched his fist. "They destroyed the gift we bestowed upon them, and all Trident did was draw it again. I would have destroyed them all for what they had done!

"I took the pen, Jimmy. I would have re-created the world, but it wouldn't work for me. It will only work for Lord Trident or someone from his bloodline. Someone like you … and of course the Shadow. I believe you have met. You see, when the original four defeated Tyranacus, Trident needed a way to control the beast. Using a piece from each of the elders, they created four bloodlines who would carry their powers and traits. You, Jimmy Threepwood, are a descendent of Lord Trident."

The inside of Jimmy's cloak started to burn where it pressed against his skin.

"I see you were given the watch by Mr Gibbs," the Gatekeeper said.

Reaching into his pocket, Jimmy removed the watch, which was hot as fire, and dangled it by its chain. It glittered as it spun around. The four engraved letters glowed fiery red on the back. DOLT.

Descendent of Lord Trident

"Join me, Jimmy Threepwood. You are the most powerful of them all. With you wielding the Rose Pen, we could create the word in our image. We could destroy the elders and rewrite the world as it should be."

Jimmy's eye started to glow. "And what of the Shadow?"

"He will be no match for us. He is weak, but I still need him for now. I've waited centuries, collected every one of you from you homes in the hope you would come to see my way of thinking, and at long last, I found one. But then I met you. "Join me, Jimmy, we can rewrite the world."

Putting the watch back inside his cloak, his hands ignited with electricity. Jimmy glanced back at Talula, unconscious on the floor behind him, and Percy resting on a bed of rubble. "For what you have done to me, Gatekeeper, you won't be leaving this room alive."

CHAPTER 43

Jimmy leapt forward in a flash, leaving a trail of fire smouldering in his wake. Slashing and stabbing wildly, the electric-charged blades sizzled through the air.

But the Gatekeeper seemed to slow the very fabric of time as he dodged and weaved, narrowly escaping the blades. As he ducked, the Gatekeeper barely avoided losing his head as the pointed tip of the blade sliced through his cowl. He slammed Jimmy in the chest with both palms hard enough to break ribs.

Jimmy flew backwards, skidding across the floor, holding his bruised side.

The Gatekeeper awarded himself a triumphant grin as he held his right arm out to the side. From the nether regions of his domain, a long-handled scythe materialised in his hand. An amethyst light glimmered over the curved blade, illuminating its razor-sharp edge.

The Gatekeeper stomped forward, twirling the mystical weapon. Sparks flew each time the blade struck the ground.

Jimmy dived forward, his golden lightning blades crackling softly, and the weapons collided in a blaze of light. Pushing the Gatekeeper back, Jimmy struck again and again, each strike parried by the wooden handle of the scythe.

After blocking the second attack, the Gatekeeper caught Jimmy off balance. In one flowing motion, he swung the scythe in an arc around the back of his head and swiped Jimmy's legs out from under him.

As the blade descended, Jimmy instinctively rolled away, and it made a chink sound on the hard stone, which sent fractures off in every direction. Leaping to his feet, Jimmy could see the Gatekeeper tugging and pulling at the jammed blade. Rage burned in his stomach, and he channelled the energy it created into his arms, reforming the glowing yellow blades, though they had faded more to a lime green colour. *This is it,* he thought. *This is my chance. Even if we are all trapped here forever, the Gatekeeper won't leave this place alive.*

Green sparks crackled over his skin as he stood in half human, half phoenix form. Flames dripped from his body, turning to ash as they tumbled to the floor. The room began to shudder and shake from the enormous energy being charged. Jimmy, the eye of the storm, trembled as the magnetised rubble and boulders were slowly drawn towards him. The ground beneath his feet began to vibrate and rumble.

Jimmy finally let go. As if fired from a gun, he tore through the air.

The Gatekeeper, still trying to free his blade, could see the approaching storm. He jerked one last time, raising the weapon in front of him, but it was too late. Jimmy's lightning sword sliced straight through the scythe and into the Gatekeeper's left shoulder, dislocating it from its bony socket.

The Gatekeeper's arm went limp as he collapsed to the floor, trying to use his feet to clamber backwards whilst holding the remains of his weapon out in front of him.

Jimmy's eyes turned blood-red, and his blade became a darker tint of green. Enraged, he raised the sword high above his head and struck down with everything he had. Over and over he struck, his blade turning a darker shade of green with each strike. His muscles burned as he struck down for the sixth, seventh … and on the eighth swing, what was left of the Gatekeeper's scythe started to split.

Trapped, the Gatekeeper gritted his jagged teeth, barely able to hold his weapon up. As Jimmy raised his blade for what would surely be the final time, the Gatekeeper turned away and silently mumbled a series of words.

Out of the corner of his eye, Jimmy saw a flicker of movement. He turned to his right in time to see the headless Diamond Giant Percy had defeated bounding towards him. The giant wasn't moving like it had before, but more like a puppet on a string, controlled by a master.

Jimmy grimaced, not giving a thought to the giant's indestructible body as he waited. As the giant's shadow dropped over him, he twisted and drove the blade as hard as he could into the giant's core and let go. The sword carved straight through the giant. As it exploded out the other side, Jimmy caught the weapon in his right hand. Momentum carried the giant forward three steps, where it stopped and collapsed to the floor.

Jimmy turned back to the Gatekeeper, who was using the hilt of his battered scythe to clamber to his feet.

"You really think you can defeat me in my own world!" the Gatekeeper shouted. "I am the creator of this prison. It bends to my will!" With that, he rammed the end of the hilt hard into the stone floor.

Hundreds of round black holes materialised, and with them came the deathly screams of the imprisoned. Black, clawed hands appeared from within, used to pull out the bodies of flickering souls.

Soon, ten of them stood before Jimmy as he slowly backed away, then twenty, then a hundred, then a thousand.

Within minutes, a sea of blackness began to move in unison aggressively towards him.

CHAPTER 44

Time is up….

Jimmy ducked as the first claws slashed through the air. He used his sword to cut off the clawed hand, and the soul evaporated. Holding his hand flat, the sword morphed into a javelin. As he threw it through an approaching line, the lightning bolt skewered ten souls, which then exploded in a shower of black smoke.

Jimmy noticed a large group of souls had surrounded Talula, while even more moved slowly towards Percy and Harry. Slowing his heart rate, he calmed his thoughts. His feet lifted from the floor as he shifted to his phoenix form. Flashing forward in a blaze of fire, he flew straight through twenty creatures, leaving a trail of evaporating black smoke behind him.

Circling Talula's unconscious body, he crashed through another line of the creatures, giving her some breathing space. Exhausted, his arms felt heavy as he changed back to his human form. Jimmy watched as hundreds of souls, thousands, climbed through the floor.

There is no end! he screamed inside. No matter how many they wiped out, more crawled up to fill in the holes. In the background, he could hear the unmistakable sound of the Gatekeeper's maniacal laughter. Hundreds of the creatures were between him and the Gatekeeper.

Jimmy created a lightening sword in his battered hand as another ring of creatures took formation around him. When he felt a burning heat radiating outward from his smouldering robes, he reached in with his free hand to pull out his pocket watch. It glowed, flashing like a beacon. A few steps to his right, another, much smaller, light sparkled. Holding his sword high, Jimmy knelt to examine it, finding the ring glowing on Percy's severed index finger. The *Ring of Vision*.

The instant he pulled the ring off Percy's finger, the digit faded away, reforming on Percy's hand.

As Jimmy held the flashing ring up, his eyes glazed over, turning black, and his spirit lifted into the air, suspended a few feet off the ground. Mist covered his vision, and he offered a silent scream to his body below.

"Do not worry, Jimmy Threepwood, I only give me watches to special people," said a familiar voice from with the curtain of fog.

The fog parted as a young-looking Watchmaker wearing tiny round glasses stepped into the light, a neat bow tie against his neck, his pocket stuffed full of metal tools.

"Mr Gibbs," Jimmy said, amazed.

"Didn't I tell you that the time would come when you would need this watch, that the watch is mightier than any sword. This is that time."

"But I need to get back down there," Jimmy said, trying frantically to fight his way through the fog.

"Do not worry, Jimmy, you will protect them." Mr Gibbs moved his hand and cleared the view. Far below, Jimmy saw his body slashing and cutting through wave after wave of flickering souls. "The *Ring of Vision* belongs to Percy, but when combined with the power of the watch, it will grant you a brief glimpse into the future. Or, in your case, a glimpse of a future where you escape.

"What do you—" Before he had a chance to finish, Mr Gibbs disappeared, and a future time flashed before his eyes.

"The Ring ... the Watch," voices shouted all around him.

With a gasp, Jimmy found himself sucked back into his human body. Turning to his right, he saw it, the only means of escape. Mr Gibbs had known this would happen from the start. He had planned for it all along.

The words he had heard echoed in his mind. *'This place is only a prison for those whose time it is. None shall be kept against their TIME!'*

That's the key, Jimmy thought. None of them were supposed to be here. Slicing through another five waves, he bought himself just enough time to pull the watch chain through the ring. As he swung the watch faster and faster around his head, he stared at his fallen companions, then back at the Gatekeeper. "You survived this time, but I won't fail again," Jimmy shouted through gritted teeth.

He flung the watch through the air. As it sailed over the heads of the approaching shadows, they tried to pluck it from the sky. The watch hit the reflective surface of the glass mirror and disappeared with a plop, as though it had been thrown in a pool of deep water.

Jimmy held his breath as the reflective surface cracked, then exploded, showering the floor with glass. Like a magnetised tornado, a stream of air wrapped its invisible hands around Jimmy, Talula, Harry and Percy, pushing rubble and boulders aside as it dragged them one by one into the mirror.

The instant Percy's foot disappeared through the frame, the glass fragments leapt from the floor and were forged back together, reforming the mirror.

*

"Arghh!" the Gatekeeper screamed angrily at his army of souls, who were desperately trying to escape back into their holes. A cracking noise echoed off the cavern walls as he pushed his shoulder bone back into its socket.

"Your time is up, Jimmy Threepwood. It's far too late. No one can stop what we have started."

CHAPTER 45

The grand wooden doors to Sepura Castle exploded, leaving shards of splintered wood littered across the shiny chequered floor. Three figures entered the castle shrouded in darkness.

The Gatekeeper hovered over the threshold, drinking in in the damp, stale air as it washed over him. Pausing, he stared up to the empty platform above the wobbling staircase, remembering the elders who'd stood there laughing as he'd tried to use the Rose Pen.

"Imjimn-Ra," he snarled to the shrivelled, lifeless corpse that stood next to him. "Guard the bridge."

"Yes, Master," Imjimn-Ra replied through his leathery, toothless mouth. He turned and clambered back over the wooden slats.

The Gatekeeper unleashed a stream of black lightning which flashed through the hall and hit the wobbling staircase, where it exploded in a shower of sparks. Whips of lightning flashed across the tiles, cracking and splitting them. Floating green flames were brought crashing to the ground, igniting the tapestries and curtains, setting a corner of the castle ablaze.

"No!" a voice wheezed from the back of the castle. Majordomo clanked across the floor, his cape flapping behind him.

Standing before the Gatekeeper, the Shadow started to move, but the Gatekeeper stopped him with a gesture. "Go and get what you came for," the Gatekeeper said.

Hovering to the left of the room, the Shadow nodded.

The Gatekeeper approached Majordomo, where they stood eye to eye. "Yet again you interfere, you pathetic creature." Tightening his grip, a small obsidian knife appeared in his hand. Thrusting forward, the Gatekeeper drove the knife into Majordomo's chest. "Did you not learn from the last time you got in my way?" He twisted the knife, "Look at me!" the Gatekeeper screamed. "If you had only kept out of the way that day. If only."

The Gatekeeper turned and floated away as Majordomo collapsed to the floor.

*

The Shadow materialised on the other side of the Lorda Door. Behind his head, the purple diamond window quivered as it returned to glass.

"Hello?" a surprised voice shouted from a storage cupboard at the far end of the classroom. "The classes have finished, and only students of a certain order have acc—"

Professor Lorda backed away, bumping into the window ledge. "You! How? So, it's been you all along. You're the Shadow. You killed Professor Tinker and Madam Shrill … but why? Why are you doing this?"

"Why, you ask, my old teacher … because I have seen through the promises of the elders. I have seen through their lies … and I plan to be the ruler of this world one day. That is why." The Shadow turned his head and stared at one of the desks. "But for now, you have something I want!"

Lorda froze, following the Shadow's gaze towards the wooden desk and the mask sitting on a pile of papers and books.

Lorda dived forward, crashing into the table as it scraped along the floor. But he was too late. The Shadow, little more than a blur, grabbed the mask as the table and Lorda went sliding straight through his spirit form into the blackboard.

"Too slow, Professor," the Shadow said, the mask resting face-down on his palm.

"No, please … please, I need it. I must have the mask."

The Shadow put the mask with the menacing diagonal stripes on his face. The inky black substance snaked over his already dark features. As a foot-long nail burst through his fingers, the Shadow moved his neck around to test out his new weapon.

"Professor, you will never need anything again!"

The End

The adventure continues in:

**Jimmy Threepwood
and the
Divider of Fabric and Space.**

Thank you for choosing this book. If you enjoyed it, please consider telling your friends or leaving a review on Goodreads or the site where you bought it. Word of mouth is an author's best friend and much appreciated.

About the Author

Rich Pitman was born in Newport, South Wales. He now lives in the picturesque Forest of Dean which is situated in the western part of the county of Gloucestershire, England.

Rich is the author of the popular children's series following the life of a young boy, Jimmy Threepwood, who is one day destined to destroy the world. The first book in the five-book series is entitled *Jimmy Threepwood and the Veil of Darkness.*

Jimmy Threepwood and the Veil of Darkness was voted as a finalist for the People's Book Prize.

http://www.peoplesbookprize.com/section.php?id=7
https://www.facebook.com/jimmy.threepwood
Wordpress: http://jimmythreepwoodblog.wordpress.com/
Pinterest: https://pinterest.com/jimmythreepwood/
Twitter - @threepwoodbooks

Also by Rich Pitman

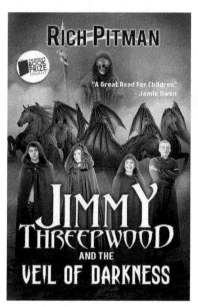

Jimmy Threepwood and the Veil of Darkness

Even heroes do bad things, but there's something really unfortunate about being selected to join the forces of evil and become one of the four horsemen of the apocalypse!

When Jimmy Threepwood is collected to face his dark destiny and destroy the world with his supernatural powers, he is faced with a choice....

What lengths will he go to for the sake of revenge?

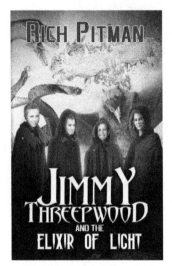

Jimmy Threepwood and the Elixir of Light

Jimmy Threepwood is a young boy with a tormented past. Having lost his father, the conspiracies against him by his dark teammates come to a head as they now face the Gatekeeper of life and death in a bid to destroy him. But Jimmy and his friends are starting to decay because of their use of dark magic and must find the fabled Elixir of Light—a mysterious compound that will restore their bodies and allow them to continue their dark mission to destroy the world.